Long Live Argalon

Edmund Tamakloe

— For Karla, dare to dream!

Ed—

For you, Elizabeth

O hail, mighty Argalon!
Long live thy holy name!
May generations to come forever know you!
May the blood spilled by our forefathers
In birthing you never go in vain!
And may all, standing in unity,
Forever defend you
Even at the cost of our lives!
Hail, mighty Argalon!
Long live thy name!

—Argalon Ode

CONTENTS

ACT ONE—THINGS FALL APART (REVELATION)

ACT TWO—AFTER THINGS FALL APART (LONG LIVE ARGALON)

ACT I—THINGS FALL APART (REVELATION)

COUP

Queen Ailith had just dismissed her attendants and was standing at the bay window of her chamber staring thoughtfully into the distance when she heard a loud knock on her door.

"You may come in, Romelot," Queen Ailith said without turning.

A tall, broad-shouldered, partially-armored guard in his late forties ran into the chamber and bowed down on the marble floor lined with fur. "Your Highness, I bring you grave news."

Romelot was Her Majesty Queen Ailith's assistant chief guard.

"No need for formalities, Romelot. You may rise, for I know why you came," Queen Ailith replied, still staring into the distance with her right side facing Romelot as the soft rays of the dying embers of the setting sun filtering through the window caressed her youthful face. In her early thirties, she was tall and slender, had long gold hair and was draped in a long white silk gown embroidered with precious stones.

Romelot rose to his feet.

Queen Ailith continued staring out the window, and after a short while, turned. "I knew this day would come," she said, a grave and forlorn look hovering on her pale face, and walked gracefully with her gown trailing behind her to the center of the chamber to a table that had a crystal ball sitting on top of it. She stroked the ball with her slender fingers and the image of a temple appeared in the ball, revealing anxious men, women, and children covered in ash gathered around her statue with olive branches in their hands and crying out about the perils that had befallen the land—about the plague sweeping through the land, killing people and livestock alike, and the failure of the land to yield its best when they plant. "Oh, how it aches my heart to see them wail like sheep without a shepherd."

"Surely, Your Highness, there must be something you can do," Romelot said, walking up to the table. "The people have great faith in you."

"I know they do, Romelot. But I'm afraid I'm no longer what I used to be; my powers fail me these days," Queen Ailith replied, and then all of a sudden, as if to demonstrate, she stretched forth her right hand, commanding the bed on the far wall to change into a cup, but the bed did not change. She commanded her mirror to change into a scroll, but instead it changed into a frog. She commanded the chest-of-drawers to change into a shoe, but instead it changed into a bowl.

"Oh my!" Romelot exclaimed.

Queen Ailith sighed and lowered her head despondently.

"What do we do now, Your Highness?"

"I shall speak to the people," Queen Ailith replied, raising her head, and asked Romelot to go summon the Chief Priest and the people to the castle courtyard from her temple which was just outside the castle. "Dutton should already be there. I sent him earlier," she added.

Dutton was Queen Ailith's chief guard.

"Aye, Your Highness," Romelot replied, bowing his head briefly, and left hastily.

Shortly after Romelot left, Queen Ailith went and sat on the edge of her bed, which was lined with gold velvet spread with leopard-spotted pillows stacked at the headboard, and buried her face in her hands. The frog croaking in the corner soon distracted her. Raising her head, she stretched forth her right hand to change the frog back to the mirror, but instead it changed to a deer. She tried again, but the deer changed to a centaur. Just as she stretched her right hand angrily in an attempt to change the centaur to the mirror, her identical twin sister

Emordra appeared into the chamber in a cloud of smoke, laughing hysterically.

"Terrific. See who comes now to torture me at my darkest hour," Queen Ailith muttered under her breath.

"Oh, poor you," Emordra said, mumbled some demented-seeming phrases and stretched forth her left hand, commanding the centaur to change back to its original item; the centaur changed back to the mirror. Wearing a victorious smile on her face, she sauntered over to Queen Ailith in her long, black satin gown, kissed her on the cheek and sat beside her on the edge of the bed; her hair strands were made of live baby boa constrictors.

Queen Ailith rose from the bed and walked up to the bay window. "Why are you here, Emordra?" she said with her side turned to Emordra.

"Why am I here?" Emordra scoffed. "I thought the great 'goddess' and queen of Argalon would have divined that easily," she added mockingly.

"Don't play games with me, Emordra. Make known your request or begone. I have pressing matters to attend to."

"Fair enough." Emordra rose from the bed. "I'm here to claim my birthright, the throne, from you."

At that, the atmosphere in the chamber grew taut like a stretched bow. Queen Ailith turned sharply at the window, a fierce look in her eyes like a lion ready to pounce. "Get out of my chamber!" she ordered, pointing to the tall gilded doorway while trying to control the anger that was beginning to surge through her like a raging sea.

"Don't make me do this the hard way, sister."

"Get out now or I'll destroy you like I should have done ten years ago when you murdered our father!"

The image of that fateful day flashed across Emordra's memory in bits and pieces. She recalled her father lying propped up in his bed, his pale face contorted from the poison that was causing him to waste away. She remembered walking up to him in his bed with tears in her eyes, seizing his throat, her fingers clenching and choking. A vague chill had descended on her afterwards; it was like something, a part of her, died that day. Queen Ailith, who had been appointed queen of Argalon moments prior by their father, had pardoned her and appointed her chief general of the armies of Argalon. Emordra could almost hear her dying father's soft pleas for her not to harm her sister as she walked up to Queen Ailith at the bay window.

"I hope you do know, sister, that you are in no position to give commands—not when your powers fail you," she said almost in a whisper.

"Try me!" Queen Ailith said, suddenly pushing Emordra back and sending her flying across the chamber with a powerful force from her palms; Emordra crashed into the opposite wall and fell to the ground.

"Break it off, sister. I'm warning you," Emordra said, staggering to her feet and grunting.

Queen Ailith stretched forth her hands; ten darts shot from the tips of her fingernails toward Emordra. Emordra did an instinctive and flexible split; the darts missed her narrowly and stitched the wall behind her.

Upon missing, Queen Ailith raised her hands and began chanting; an enormous red-winged dragon with a forked tongue came crashing through the bay window into the chamber in no time and began heading straight for Emordra. Emordra chanted too and a golden sword appeared into her hand as the dragon surged toward her. The force from the advancing dragon knocked Emordra to the ground. But after she fell, and the dragon closed in on her to devour her, she plunged her sword straight through its mouth; the dragon howled, staggered about uncontrollably like a drunkard and crashed dead into the table with the crystal ball, shattering both the table and the ball.

Queen Ailith froze in disbelief.

"Is that all you've got, sister?" Emordra rose to her feet, panting and with a fierce look in her eyes. "Now, my turn!"

Emordra swung her hair and the baby boa constrictors on her head grew, enlarging and lengthening like ropes into giant snakes, and coiled around Queen Ailith, squeezing and choking her. Queen Ailith struggled ceaselessly to free herself from the clutches of the boa constrictors, albeit vainly. Realizing she was unable to free herself, Queen Ailith played dead, but just as the boa constrictors uncoiled from around her, shortened, and returned to Emordra's head elastically, before she fell to the ground, she unleashed a dart that caught Emordra on her thigh.

"Arrgggghhh!" Emordra wailed, and realizing she had been duped, drew her golden sword from the dragon's mouth and flung it at Queen Ailith who rolled away in time to evade the vicious cut.

Queen Ailith rose to her feet afterwards, and before she could unleash another dart, Emordra cast a spell on her.

"My legs! My legs!" Queen Ailith wailed agonizingly as she fell to the ground and struggled to undo the spell.

"Look at you now, helpless and teary," Emordra teased, pulled the dart from her thigh and healed her wound. "I warned you, but you wouldn't listen."

"Guards!" Queen Ailith called out, breathless, but not a single guard responded to her call.

"Oops, did I fail to mention this was a coup taking place and that most of your guards are dead? In fact, the only guards outside now are the ones who betrayed you," Emordra said. "Here, watch. Guards!"

Romelot and a tall, lanky guard, Dagus, ran into the chamber and bowed to Emordra. "At your service, Your Highness," they chorused.

Queen Ailith was shocked to see Romelot and Dagus. Along with her chief guard Dutton, they had been her most loyal guards…or so it appeared. She grew weak in the body.

Emordra chuckled. "See? I told you, sister."

"You witch! Don't think you'll get away with this."

Emordra scoffed. "*I will.* Who would stop me? Powerless you? I don't think so." She turned to Romelot and Dagus. "Take her to the Pollyanna Forest where she is to spend the rest of her days as an outcast, banished from our world forever."

"Aye, Your Highness," Romelot and Dagus chorused, rose and seized Queen Ailith.

"Take your hands off me, treacherous creatures!" Queen Ailith exploded, pushing Romelot and Dagus.

Romelot and Dagus seized her from the floor nonetheless.

"This is not over, Emordra! You'll live to regret this!" Queen Ailith said, resisting fiercely as Romelot and Dagus hoisted her up and exited the chamber.

JAILED

"What did she promise you? Lands? Castles? Women? Is that how much your honor is worth?" Queen Ailith said, still struggling to free herself as Romelot and Dagus walked down a spiral marble staircase with her still hoisted up.

"We did what was best for Argalon," Romelot replied.

Queen Ailith scoffed. "You should both be ashamed of—"

"Shut up!" Dagus exploded, threatening to drop her onto the staircase and drag her.

Queen Ailith became silent—albeit reluctantly.

Within a short while, they descended the stairs into a hall with walls overlaid with gold and came across Dutton; he was on his way back from the temple and was wielding a blood-splattered sword in his right hand, a result of him having to battle traitorous guards inside the courtyard after reentering the castle grounds.

"Put Her Majesty down now!" Dutton commanded, stepping in front of Romelot and Dagus upon seeing Queen Ailith hoisted up.

Wearing a leather sandals and a white robe speckled with blood, Dutton was tall, well-built, dark-skinned and in his early forties.

"You are no longer in command," Romelot replied. "Step aside or die."

"Sheathe your sword, Dutton," Queen Ailith interrupted.

"I can't, Your Majesty. My lot is to defend you."

"This is not your fight; it's mine."

"I would listen to her if I were you," Dagus interrupted.

"Your fight is *always* my fight," Dutton replied, and once again ordered Romelot and Dagus to put Queen Ailith down or feel the wrath of his blood-splattered blade upon their flesh.

Romelot and Dagus scoffed.

"You have given me no choice," Dutton said, immediately running and lunging at Dagus and drawing blood from his arm.

Screaming in pain, Dagus and Romelot dropped Queen Ailith to the floor, drew their swords and began fighting Dutton.

"Don't fight, Dutton. You'll not win; treacherous guards have taken over the castle," Queen Ailith said from the floor, grunting in pain.

"It's my honor and duty to defend you, even without victory in sight," Dutton replied, fending off Romelot's attack and locking swords with Dagus. With their swords locked together, Dutton kneed Dagus in his stomach, pushed him to the ground and plunged his sword into his neck.

Seeing Dagus dead, Romelot became incensed and, uttering a shrill cry, lunged at Dutton. Dutton swerved, turned and stepped Romelot in the back; Romelot fell face-down to the ground, rose again, and uttering another shrill cry, came running toward Dutton.

The fierce clanging of swords began drawing guards from around the castle.

"Run, Your Majesty! Save Yourself!" Dutton said, panting, as he stepped Romelot to the ground once more and braced himself for the dozen guards rushing onto the scene to join the fight.

After a bit of hesitation, Queen Ailith crawled agonizingly through a nearby doorway and disappeared from sight.

"Follow her!" Romelot ordered after rising from the ground; a couple of guards chased after Queen Ailith while the rest joined in the fight against Dutton.

The ensuing mayhem soon drew Emordra onto the scene. "Stop! Sheathe your swords!" she commanded from the balcony overlooking the hall.

The guards who had all closed in on Dutton stopped, turned and looked up.

"Why this melee? What's going on here?" Emordra asked.

"This vagrant tried to stop us from taking Ailith away as Your Highness commanded," Romelot replied breathlessly, pointing his sword to Dutton who had his sword pinned to the neck of one of the guards.

"Why am I not surprised?" Dutton said to Emordra, equally breathless. "I suspected you were behind this."

"Ah, the chief guard himself. Or should I say former?" Emordra said with a mocking smile on her face, turned, sauntered down the nearby stairs and walked up to Dutton as the guards gave way. "For ten good years I tried to woo you to my cause, but you wouldn't give in, pledging undying loyalty to my worthless sister instead."

"I only fight for just causes," Dutton replied.

"Is my cause not just?"

"What justice is there in betraying your father's dying wish that your sister rules Argalon?"

"Nonsense! My father's true wish was for me to rule Argalon instead of Ailith. But you connived with her and convinced my father to do otherwise."

"You know very well that's not true."

15

"Do you call me a liar, Dutton? Do you?" Emordra moved closer to Dutton, a fierce look in her eyes as the snakes began writhing on her head.

"Still your tongue, Dutton, or she'll have you killed," Queen Ailith interrupted; she had been captured and brought back to the scene by the guards who had gone after her.

"Your Highness, she tried to escape," one of the guards who brought Queen Ailith back said.

Emordra scoffed. "You think you can escape?" she said to Queen Ailith and then turned and ordered Dutton to drop his sword or have her killed before his eyes.

Glancing at Queen Ailith who was being held by two guards and the rest of the guards around the hall, Dutton hesitated, and then dropped his sword.

"Good. I can see that your loyalty to my sister is steadfast," Emordra said and then ordered the guards to seize Dutton and take him and Queen Ailith to the castle dungeon, securing the gate with as many guards as possible.

Romelot walked up to Emordra as a couple of guards moved to seize Dutton. "Don't you want Ailith taken to the Pollyanna Forest anymore, Your Highness?"

"I want her close so I can keep my eyes on her and that insidious guard of hers."

As the guards took Queen Ailith and Dutton away, a short and muscular guard, Gazan, walked up to Romelot and Emordra, bowed and informed Emordra that the citizenry were beginning to gather in the castle courtyard.

"Who summoned them?" Emordra asked.

"Your sister, I believe," Gazan replied, rising.

"Right."

"Should I go disband them, Your Highness?" Gazan asked.

"No, I shall address them and inform them of the change of regime," Emordra replied.

"I'm not sure that's the best thing to do now, Your Highness," Romelot interrupted.

"Why not?"

"I fear the people would riot, for they love Ailith."

"Well, someone has to tell them sooner or later that Ailith is no more."

"True, but at an opportune time."

"Now is the fitting time," Emordra replied. "Lead me to the people."

"As you wish, Your Highness," Romelot replied and he and Gazan led Emordra outside to the citizenry.

ESCAPES

The citizenry gathered in the castle courtyard were engaged in raucous conversations amongst themselves when Emordra walked out onto the balcony overlooking the courtyard, flanked on both sides by Romelot and Gazan.

The evening sky above was bathed in an orange and pink glow as the ever-retreating sun made its usual slow and glorious bow to the impending night. From the balcony of the castle, which was perched high atop the towering Cova Mountain like an imposing statue, one could see the majestic and picturesque city of Aravon, nestled comfortably between the arms of lagoons and lakes, spread out beneath. Also, one could see numerous boats docked along the coast of the Nubian Ocean bordering Argalon to the south.

Emordra raised her hand from the balcony, motioning for silence; the people grew quiet upon noticing her. "Noble citizens of Argalon, I greet you in peace and harmony," she said.

"Where is the queen?" a gray-haired old man, the Chief Priest, who was responsible for leading worship at the temple, immediately interrupted from the front as the people began murmuring amongst themselves, for they were startled to see Emordra addressing them instead of Queen Ailith or Dutton whom Queen Ailith usually sent to address them whenever she was unable to.

"Yes, where is Her Majesty or Dutton?" another person interjected from the back of the crowd.

Emordra motioned for silence. "I bear grave and sad news for you, Argalon—Ailith is no more."

"What do you mean she is no more?" the Chief Priest asked. "She just summoned us over," he added as the people began murmuring again.

Emordra raised her hands once more, motioning for silence and the people grew quiet again. "There has been a change in regime—I am your new queen and ruler!"

"Booooooooooooooooooo!" the people jeered, some erupting into vociferous chants, saying, 'We want Queen Ailith! We want Queen

Ailith!' Others picked up pebbles scattered around the courtyard and began pelting Emordra.

Romelot and Gazan stepped in front of Emordra, shielding her from the pebble attack, and shepherded her back into the castle.

"Miscreants! They better get used to me because I'm going to be their queen for the foreseeable future," Emordra said as soon as she was safe in the castle. "Disband them with whips, Romelot and Gazan, and do not spare even the little ones among them. That should teach them a lesson for their insolence."

"Yes, Your Highness," Romelot and Gazan chorused and went back outside immediately.

Meanwhile, the noise echoing in the courtyard reached the dungeon where Queen Ailith and Dutton were being held captive.

"Do you hear them?" Dutton said, rising to his feet from the rough concrete floor he and Queen Ailith had been sitting on as the chants for 'we want Queen Ailith!' reached them. "They chant your name," he added as a couple of rats squealed and scurried past his shackled feet into a hole.

"What good are their chants?" Queen Ailith replied in resignation. "That's not going to stop my sister from doing whatever she wants."

"Look at the bright side, Your Majesty."

Queen Ailith scoffed. "And what might that bright side be? That I'm in prison, and my conscienceless sister sits on my throne?"

"No. What I mean is that you still have the hearts of the people. They are loyal to you, and that means Emordra's illegal regime, no matter how well she tries to fashion it, cannot prevail."

"You of all people should know that my sister is a beguiling serpent and gets whatever she wants regardless of whatever means she has to employ in the process."

"She will not have her way this time—not if I can get you out of here in time to stop her in her tracks and save Argalon from impending ruin."

"And how would you do that?" Queen Ailith said, tugging on the shackles binding her and Dutton as if to remind him that they were in chains.

Dutton stared into Queen Ailith's deep blue eyes briefly and then suddenly fell to the ground and started convulsing, foaming at the mouth and thrashing his limbs about violently as his eyes rolled into their sockets.

Queen Ailith, who was not sure about what was going on, became frightened. "Duton? Duton? Help! Somebody help! He's dying!" she shouted as she pulled vainly on the chains that bound her hands.

Within a short while, the iron gate to the dungeon flew open and two guards stormed in. The guards caught sight of Dutton convulsing, ran over, and began undoing the shackles from his arms and legs.

Dutton immediately kicked the guard who undid the last chain from his leg, reached for the second guard's dagger from his side and plunged it into his side. Before the first guard could react by drawing his sword, Dutton stabbed him in his neck.

Queen Ailith looked on, stunned at the rapidity with which Dutton had killed the guards. Of course, she knew he was an excellent guard, but he always never ceased to amaze her.

The noise from the fight drew a third guard from outside, however. Apparently, he had been standing guard at the gate. But the guard immediately turned and ran back out like a startled dog the moment he ran in and caught sight of his colleagues lying dead on the ground.

"We've got to get out of here," Dutton said breathlessly, reached for the keys from the shackles, undid Queen Ailith's chains from her legs and feet, and afterwards, put Queen Ailith onto his back as she could not walk and ran out of dungeon.

PURSUED

Emordra was so deeply engrossed with the map of the Kingdom of Argalon she was studying on the wall of her father's study that she did not notice when Romelot walked in. Of course, having served as chief general of Argalon before she instigated the coup, she had seen the map on several occasions. But now that she was queen of Argalon, a dream she had borne in her heart from the time she was a girl, the map appeared to have taken on a mythical appearance like some strange sea creature she was encountering for the first time. She could not believe she was to preside over the twelve provinces that comprised the kingdom of Argalon! Romelot watched as she ran her fingers across the map, which was carved into the wall, in a titillating manner from east to west and from north to south like a lover caressing a loved one.

"Has it sunk in yet?" Romelot interrupted after a short while.

Startled, Emordra turned and smiled when she noticed it was Romelot. "Pardon?"

"The fact that you are now queen of Argalon. Has it sunk in yet?"

"Not quite," she replied. "I always thought this moment was going to be perfect and filled with a rush of emotions. But I feel nothing. Nothing at all."

"Give it time," Romelot replied.

Emordra scoffed. "Time? How long?"

"I don't know," Romelot replied. "But I'm sure it will begin to sink in at some point, perhaps when you do get the chance to parade the streets of Argalon and hear the people shout unanimously 'hail queen of Argalon.'"

"Ah, the people—right, the people…" she paused, turning to look at her father's statue which stood beside a shelf loaded with scrolls in the far corner: he was standing erect and had his arms stretched out in a welcoming fashion. She could almost hear him telling her in his soft voice how government was all about the people, and how a ruler, no matter how great, was never greater than the people or the land he ruled. She had never liked him because she felt he was too strict on rules and loved her sister Ailith more. "Did you disband them?" she asked.

"Gazan and a handful of guards are taking care of that as we speak, Your Highness."

She turned to face Romelot. "That's a mistake, isn't it?"

"Not at all… I mean on the one hand you do not want to alienate them as no government can subsist without its people, but on the other hand you cannot allow them to become unruly and uncontrollable so soon in your administration."

"Right," Emordra replied, nodding. "But after such fractious beginning, how can I ever get them to chant 'hail queen of Argalon' across the kingdom when already they hate me? How do I win their hearts?"

"Every heart is winnable, Your Highness. How one goes about it is all that matters."

"What then do you suggest I do to win their hearts?"

"Feasts and games."

"Feasts and games?"

"Yes. As Your Highness knows the people love feasts and pageantry. In that light, I suggest you host a feast here at the castle and invite them over for entertainment, including a special time of wild games at the *Vogumgata*."

The *Vogumgata* was an arena where Argalonians hosted games of blood and gore along with occasional joust tournaments.

"Brilliant," Emordra said, a bright smile lighting up on her face. "All right then. Send my orders to the chief cook to start making preparations for the feast to be hosted at sundown tomorrow..."

"Aye, Your Highness."

"...I want every household in the city invited..."

"Aye, Your Highness."

"...And also, send word to the herald to prepare the acrobats and the dancers for the feast. And you, prepare your finest men to deliver to the people a pre-feast melee at the *Vogumga*--"

They were interrupted by the sound of the emergency bell echoing loudly through the castle.

Romelot placed his hand on the hilt of the sheathed sword on his side.

"Is that the emergency bell I hear?" Emordra asked.

"I suppose so, Your Highness," Romelot replied. "May I have your permission to go make inquiries?"

"Certainly."

As Romelot turned to leave, the guard who had ran into the dungeon earlier and ran back out upon seeing his dead comrades, ran into the chamber and bowed before Emordra.

"Speak," Emordra said, a bit impatiently.

"Ailith and Dutton have escaped from the dungeon, Your Highness," the guard said breathlessly, raising his head.

"What? How is that possible?"

"My apologies, Your Highness," the guard said and went on to narrate to Emordra how Dutton had thrown a pretentious fit, killed the guards who entered the dungeon to assist him and how he was the only one who escaped.

"You should have gone after them instead of coming to inform me," Emordra said and requested the guard's sword.

The guard, knowing what would happen should he give his sword, began pleading for his life.

Unwilling to show mercy, Emordra angrily reached for the guard's sword from his side and thrust it into his neck, saying, "I hate incompetent guards." Afterwards, she turned to Romelot who had been waiting. "What are you waiting for? Go seek them out! I want every segment of the castle barricaded! I want them brought to me dead or alive!"

"Yes, Your Highness," Romelot replied and rushed out of the chamber.

Shortly after Romelot left, Emordra, fuming, walked up to the bay window and stood there looking at the twilight sky while wearing a troubling look on her face. She knew that Queen Ailith and Dutton's escape could spell doom for her young regime and that she could not let that happen. As she stood at the window pondering her next move, she caught sight of what appeared to be a flying carpet with Dutton and Queen Ailith riding on it. "Rabbits can run, but they can't hide," she muttered, a sinister grin creeping onto her face.

Opening the bay window, she raised her hands, closed her eyes and began chanting. A number of large scorpion-like creatures with bat wings exited her mouth and began pursuing the flying carpet. Afterwards, she stood at the window watching as Dutton stood on the carpet and began having a go at the creatures with his sword as they closed in upon them. Noticing that Dutton was gaining the upper hand, Emordra chanted again; a pair of large wings sprouted on her back, and she flew out through the window after Queen Ailith and Dutton.

CAT AND MOUSE GAME

"Emordra is behind us and I can no longer contain the *Chirops*, Your Majesty!" Dutton said as he continued swinging at the scorpion-like creatures. "What shall we do?"

"I have little to no power left, Dutton," Queen Ailith replied, and then turned the flying carpet eastward toward the Elgorn Forest, which, bordered by the Elgorn River, loomed ahead of and below them, stark and foreboding and covered in a heavy mist and an inscrutable gloom.

"Where are we headed?" Dutton asked as if he could not tell where they were headed.

"The Elgorn Forest," Queen Ailith replied.

"The Forbidden Forest? There are Megaloths there!"

The guardians of the Elgorn Forest, Megaloths were towering, two-legged soul-sucking creatures with long proboscis.

"We either take our chances with them or die now."

Emordra, who had read Queen Ailith and Dutton's intents, unleashed a series of fireballs; Queen Ailith swerved the carpet; the fireballs missed them narrowly. Emordra unleashed another fireball, and as Queen Ailith swerved the carpet this time around, the fireball caught the tail of the carpet; the carpet began burning and spiraling out of control.

"We are going downnnnnnnnn!" Queen Ailith screamed as she struggled to regain control of the carpet, which was blazing and plummeting. "We have to jump," she added after realizing she was fighting a losing battle.

Dutton swung his sword at the last *Chirop* pursuing them and they both leapt off the carpet into the river.

Shortly after crashing into the river, Dutton emerged onto the surface, panting. Taking in big gulps of air, he scanned the surface of the water for Queen Ailith; she was nowhere to be found.

"Your Majesty? Your Majesty? Where are you?" Dutton called out frantically; there was still no sign of Queen Ailith. He was about to dive back under to go in search of Queen Ailith when he noticed a rippling motion on the surface of the water and caught sight of a giant water snake heading toward him. Frightened, he somersaulted in the river and began swimming away furiously.

Emordra, who had flown down with her wings folded on her back, stood watching from the riverbank opposite the Elgorn Forest as the snake rose from the water, darted at Dutton, snapped its mouth shut and crashed back into the water. For a moment, there was no sign of Dutton and the snake. Emordra was surprised when Dutton resurfaced on the water moments later, panting; the snake had missed him narrowly. She was about to go after him when the snake reemerged out of the water and seized him, coiling around his waist and squeezing. She looked on happily as Dutton struggled to free himself. The snake had pulled its head back and shot at Dutton when Dutton successfully freed his hand, pulled his dagger from his side and plunged it into the snake's right eye. Uttering a piercing hiss, the snake released Dutton and disappeared under the water, leaving blood spewing onto the surface.

With Emordra fuming on the bank, Dutton took in a large gulp of air, dove back down and went in search of Queen Ailith. After several strokes and intense searching, he found her lying on the riverbed; she was unresponsive. Without hesitation, he grabbed hold of Queen Ailith, swam back to the surface and then out of the river to the riverbank, the edge of the Elgorn Forest, and tried to resuscitate her by pressing on her chest frantically.

"Breathe, Your Majesty, breathe!" Dutton said, panting, as he continued pressing on Queen Ailith's chest feverishly.

A short while later, Queen Ailith responded, coughing out water.

"Alive! You're alive!"

"Where is she?" Queen Ailith asked as she came to herself.

Dutton pointed to Emordra across the river; Queen Ailith sat up and stared across the river at Emordra.

"Why is she not coming after us?" Dutton asked.

"Perhaps because father warned us to never venture the Elgorn Forest," Queen Ailith replied, and in that moment, they were interrupted by a very loud trumpeting roar echoing from the Elgorn Forest behind them. "Megaloth," Queen Ailith said, looking over her shoulder.

Sensing an opportunity, Emordra took to the skies and flew toward them.

Dutton scrambled to his feet after catching sight of Emordra heading toward them, put Queen Ailith onto his back and ran into the Elgorn Forest.

Laughing hysterically, Emordra made a u-turn as she got to the edge of the forest and flew back toward the castle, saying, "May the Megaloths have your souls for dinner!"

THE ELGORN FOREST I
(ENCOUNTERS WITH THE UNUSUAL KINDS)

Queen Ailith and Dutton had hardly entered into the Elgorn Forest when she requested that Dutton put her down.

"Why, Your Majesty? You can't walk."

"I feel strength in my legs."

"You what?" Dutton said, putting Queen Ailith down.

Queen Ailith did not fall to the ground like Dutton had expected and began taking steps on her own.

"It can't be," Dutton said, astonished.

"I think the forest has healing powers," Queen Ailith remarked.

Dutton drew the dagger from his side and ran it through his left palm, cutting himself.

"What are you doing?" Queen Ailith asked, shocked.

"Testing your theory," Dutton replied, as he and Queen Ailith watched the wound heal in astonishment. "The forest *does* have healing powers."

"What else can this forest do?" Queen Ailith said almost in a hushed voice, and she and Dutton turned and began walking gingerly, their eyes darting about as if they were expecting something to happen.

The forest that was bathed in mists moments earlier now seemed clear and alive with strange sounds. The waxing gibbous moon crouching in the night sky like a one-eyed dragon shone brightly through the tree canopies, lighting their path. They had just rounded a group of sequoia trees when the ground began growing mushy beneath their feet, turning into a soggy mud that started swallowing them up.

"Oh, no, what have we here?" Dutton said, struggling to gain his balance, as they both started sinking.

"A hungry mud," Queen Ailith replied, quickly steadying herself and relaxing. She had experienced a similar situation when she was ten. She, Emordra and her parents, King Debusis and Queen Zev, had gone hunting in the Pollyanna Forest on a warm afternoon when they got caught in a titanic mud that started swallowing up their horses. It was her father's wits that saved them then, and since then she knew to never resist whenever she found herself caught up in the mouth of a hungry mud.

Dutton, who was still fighting the mud, continued sinking.

"Stay calm. Don't resist," Queen Ailith said.

After a brief struggle, Dutton relaxed and stopped sinking. "How did you know what to do?"

"Father taught me so," Queen Ailith said, turned slowly, stretched, grabbed onto a nearby root jutting out from the ground and pulled herself out of the mud. Afterwards, holding onto the root for support, she offered her right hand to Dutton who grabbed it and pulled himself from the mud.

The ground immediately hardened after Dutton crawled out.

"What a strange place," Dutton said.

"The mythical Elgorn Forest. I guess we now know what it's like," Queen Ailith said, and in that moment, they were interrupted by a sudden loud trumpeting cry. Turning, they caught sight of a Megaloth standing about ten feet away from them.

Dutton instinctively pulled Queen Ailith behind him, shielding her with his muddied body.

They both had inklings about what was about to transpire. They had heard countless horror stories of Megaloths sucking the souls of people who entered the Elgorn Forest and afterwards mutilated and disemboweled them. How true those stories were, they were not sure as nobody who entered the Elgorn Forest out of accident or foolhardiness ever made it back out alive. Notwithstanding that, fear blitzed through them at the sight of the towering creature.

Queen Ailith and Dutton began taking slow steps backwards with their eyes fixed on the Megaloth, pondering their escape. As if having read their minds, the Megaloth let out another trumpeting cry, raised one of its legs up like a horse throwing a fit and slammed its proboscis on the ground; the ground reverberated like during an earthquake and the tree Queen Ailith and Dutton stood beside broke and slammed beside them, narrowly missing them. They both froze for a moment and then suddenly turned and began running; the Megaloth chased after them, hopping. With their legs covered in mud, their bodies felt heavy as they ran. Within a short while, the Megaloth closed in on them and swung its proboscis; Queen Ailith and Dutton dove to the ground and the Megaloth's trunk swept above them, barely missing. Realizing they were still alive, they staggered up and started running again with the Megaloth chasing them.

As they ran, three additional Megaloths approached them from the front, encircling and trapping them. With nowhere to run, they halted, panting in fear.

"They are going to suck our souls. What do we do?" Queen Ailith said, breathless, and suddenly stretched her hands to release spears, but there was no power in her. She tried again, chanting, but still there was no power. "Bullocks!" she cursed in frustration as she and Dutton's eyes darted back and forth from between the Megaloths and the surrounding for an escape route.

Having encircled Queen Ailith and Dutton, the Megaloths raised their trunks and touched them to one another's, creating an energy field that was growing by the second and engulfing them.

"There!" Dutton suddenly said, pointing to a large hole to his right.

Before the energy field could fully engulf them, Queen Ailith and Dutton ran and jumped into the hole, which sent them crashing into a shallow pond in a pitch black underground cave. They had hardly begun catching their breath after landing in the dark cave, however, when they caught sight of a glowing three-legged creature coming toward them.

"Just when I thought we were safe," Queen Ailith said, panting, and she and Dutton began scanning the cave for an opening as the three-legged creature closed in on them; there was none except the hole through which they had entered the cave.

Dutton drew his dagger from his side and thrust it into the creature's throat when it lunged at him and Queen Ailith. The creature uttered a queer cry and died as hot bright-green fluid spouted out of its throat. Thinking that was the end, Queen Ailith and Dutton were surprised when the

creature came back to life at the same time as about ten or more of the same type of creatures began appearing from all over the cave and advancing toward them. Dutton seized Queen Ailith's hand and they both ran and climbed back out of the opening they had fallen through earlier.

The Megaloths were nowhere in sight when they emerged out of the cave.

"Vera, that was close!" Queen Ailith said as she and Dutton lay on their backs at the entrance to the cave, trying to catch their breath.

Vera was the Argalonian goddess of love and war.

"Very close," Dutton replied. "*Now*, we do know what the Elgorn Forest is really like," he added and he and Queen Ailith laughed. A short while later, they rose up and began walking through the creepy darkness of the forest albeit vigilantly while looking for a suitable place, if any, to camp for the night. They eventually settled for the comfortable arms of the roots of a sequoia tree.

"What an evening!" Queen Ailith said as she and Dutton lay on their backs, taking in the cool night air with a blazing campfire between them.

"I always thought Emordra was capable, but I never thought she would," Dutton replied, adding that he was surprise Queen Ailith never saw everything coming, considering her ability to foresee the future.

"I *did* see it coming…the coup, the Elgorn Forest, the chaos…"

Dutton sat up, surprised. "Why didn't you prevent it then?"

Queen Ailith scoffed. "You think I never tried?" She sat up. "The truth, however, is that none of us can choose our destiny, Dutton, and none of us can change it. The more you try to change it, the more you fulfill it because every choice you make is wrapped up in fate."

"How does it all end then?"

"I don't know. I only saw glimpses."

"Glimpses?"

"My powers only show me bits and pieces of the future when I'm involved."

"You mean the powers that you no longer have?"

"Right."

For a moment there was silence between them. Dutton broke the silence asking Queen Ailith how come she no longer had her powers when Emordra still had hers and appeared even stronger and powerful.

"I really don't know. My powers began failing mysteriously few moons ago with the onset of the plague."

They were interrupted by wolves howling in the distance; Dutton asked Queen Ailith whether she was hungry.

"I am," Queen Ailith replied.

"Should I go hunt, Your Majesty?"

"No, for we know not what additional surprises lie in wait behind this blanket of darkness," Queen Ailith replied. "The night is already far spent. Let us sleep. Come morning we shall hunt."

"Sleep then, Your Majesty. I shall keep watch over you."

"You have done too much for me this day, Dutton, and I cannot begin to express to you my gratitude for your loyalty and the risks you took to protect me. I am grateful and could not ask for more. Sleep. I shall be fine."

"Alright then, good night, Your Majesty," Dutton said and he and Queen Ailith lied back in the tree's arms.

"Good night, Dutton."

THE ELGORN FOREST II
(MORE ENCOUNTERS WITH THE UNUSUAL KINDS)

When Dutton woke in the morning, Queen Ailith was nowhere to be found. Surprised, he staggered to his feet and began looking around while calling out to her frantically.

"Your Majesty? Your Majesty? Where are you?"

There was no response.

When he did not hear any response, Dutton began searching around the forest anxiously for Queen Ailith. He had not gone far from where they slept, when he came across an opening leading out of the forest. Walking through the opening, he discovered a river in which Queen Ailith was bathing with her back facing him. Uttering a sigh of relief, Dutton walked up and went and stood on the riverbank, watching Queen Ailith bathe, as the soft rays of the rising sun caressed her young and voluptuous body.

"You are awake," Queen Ailith said when she eventually turned and caught sight of Dutton standing on the riverbank.

"My apologies for the intrusion, Your Majesty," Dutton said, trying to look away in embarrassment after Queen Ailith caught his eye.

"I never said you were intruding," Queen Ailith replied. "Come on. Join me."

"I beg your pardon, Your Majesty?"

"You heard me."

"But Your Majesty, it's not fitting—"

"*I* get to decide what's fitting."

"Yes, but—"

"Are you going to disobey the order of your queen?"

Dutton stood on the riverbank, starring at Queen Ailith's fair body. For the fifteen years he had served at the castle while watching her grow into a full-fledged woman and become queen after the death of her father, he had always had feelings for her but kept them chained up as she had taken a vow of spinsterhood. Her perky and succulent-looking breasts began arousing those old feelings within him once more as he stared at her in the river. The animal in him wanted to give in to her call, but the guard he was cautioned, for he knew that life was never going to be the same again between them should he give in.

"Are you *really* going to disobey the order of your queen?" Queen Ailith asked once more.

Slowly and reluctantly, Dutton took off his mud-caked robe and dagger, laid them on the riverbank beside Queen Ailith's gown and joined her in the river, albeit staying far off as possible.

"Come closer, Dutton. I won't bite."

"I feel very uncomfortable, Your Majesty."

"Don't be silly. Is this your first time seeing a naked woman?"

"Not that, Your Majesty."

"Then what?"

"You are the queen of Argalon."

"Put off your guard, Dutton, and join me in play," Queen Ailith replied and began swimming away. "Catch me if you can."

Hesitating briefly, Dutton dove after Queen Ailith as he was not one to often pass off a challenge. After a few strokes, he caught up to Queen Ailith and grabbed hold of her leg. "I've caught you," he said, breathless, as they both floated in the river facing each other.

"Only because I let you," Queen Ailith replied, equally breathless, and moved closer to Dutton, staring intently into his brown eyes. "I've never been naked and alone with a male before."

"I've never been naked with a queen in a river before," Dutton replied.

Queen Ailith smiled, closed in on Dutton, and just as she was about to kiss him on his lips, they heard a loud, squeaky cry above them. Lifting their heads, they caught sight of a fleet of large predatory birds flying toward them.

"Under!" Dutton said, and he and Queen Ailith took in deep gulps of air and dove underwater.

The creatures came and circled above the water for a while and then disappeared. A short while after, Queen Ailith and Dutton rose from underwater and, taking in gulps of air, looked around for the creatures. After making sure the creatures were nowhere in sight, they both swam out of the river to the bank to put on their garments.

As they stood on the bank wearing their garments, however, a group of snarling two-legged creatures with horns on their foreheads, wielding spears and bows and arrows, advanced out of the forest toward them. Dutton pulled Queen Ailith closer to him and picked up his dagger.

"Don't come any closer," Dutton said waving his dagger back and forth at the advancing creatures; the creatures kept on coming—undaunted.

"Should we run?" Queen Ailith whispered.

"They would kill us if we try to," Dutton replied.

"They'll kill us anyway," Queen Ailith replied, stepped the first creature that came closer to them, and Dutton plunged his dagger into its chest.

Seeing their comrade dead, the rest of the creatures descended angrily upon Dutton and Queen Ailith and seized them...

THE VOGUMGATA

The men, women and children of the city of Aravon turned out in great numbers on the *Vogumgata*. The noise reverberating from the arena floated on the cool, crisp breeze blowing about and could be heard as far as the province of Sud, one of the twelve provinces comprising the Kingdom of Argalon. Not even the midday sun, briefly obscured by a group of gray lenticular clouds dragging lazily in the sky could outshine the titanic structure of the *Vogumgata*.

Built during the fourth year of the reign of Degas, Argalon's first and greatest ruler who led an audacious slave rebellion against King Jujides of the North, eventually leading to the birth of Argalon as a kingdom, the *Vogumgata* had served as the gateway to the afterlife for many warriors, both strong and weak, who had the opportunity to grace its holy sands. Nicknamed "The Theatre of Dreams," the

Vogumgata lived and breathed in the hearts and minds of the Argalonians.

As part of the pregame festivities, the jugglers and magicians took to the sands of the arena, performing various stunts. Emordra, who was sitting high up at the *Petiola*, the section reserved for dignitaries, looked on in satisfaction when one of the magicians pulled an enormous Argalonian flag on a flagstaff out of his ear and began running around the arena, waving the flag back and forth. The flag was red and white and had a fully armored knight riding on a horse with a sword stretched before him. The words "Liberty, Equality, and Justice" were inscribed on the bottom of the flag in the *santicrit* language widely spoken across the kingdom.

"Yaaaaa," the people, who were standing on their feet, cheered and clapped as the magician made rounds in the arena.

They were interrupted when the *Vogan*, or king of drums, suddenly cried an enormous cry from the center of the arena.

The crowd went wild as a group of acrobats, accompanied by a sextet of well adorned women wearing green sashes around their waists along with brass wire gauntlets on their elbows and ankles, emerged out of the dugout into the center of the arena and began performing various flips and dances. Not even Emordra could contain her excitement at the beautiful spectacle. Wearing a beaming smile on her face, she rose to her feet in her sultry red gown and began clapping from the *Petiola* with Romelot, Gazan and a handful of attendants standing guard behind her. She did not care that the dignitaries she had invited to the event from around the city did not come. This was the day she was going to win the hearts of the people and that was all that mattered, she thought to herself satisfactorily as she clapped. She was going to give them spectacle and blood and they were going to love her for it....

At last the moment came that everybody who had gathered at the *Vogumgata* had been waiting for. The *Vogan* cried once more, and as the acrobats, jugglers, magicians and women exited the arena, an announcer, a hefty man wearing a white cloth that was passed under his right armpit and fastened on his left shoulder, took to the center of the arena.

"Argalon, are you ready for the games?" the announcer shouted.

"Yeeeessssssssssssssssss!" the people roared.

The announcer gestured toward the dugout, and immediately, a knight, accompanied by ten fully armored *Vogums* or jousters, rode out of the dugout into the arena on horsebacks.

The people, who were under the impression that they were going to be treated to gladiator-like ghoulish fights, were left disappointed when they came to notice they were going to be treated to jousts instead. (Originally, the *Vogumgata* had been built for jousts, but that soon changed when more and more prisoners of war and outlaws were condemned to death on its sands).

"Boooooooooooo!" the people jeered the announcer and began pelting him with fruits.

Shifting uncomfortably in her seat, Emordra became disconcerted at the sights.

The announcer motioned for calm among the people, and when they eventually quieted down and stopped pelting him, he informed them that Bavarus was to partake in the tournament.

Bavarus, who had been the undefeated joust champion for the past three decades, held a special place in the hearts of the people because he defeated the notorious Radus in a breathtaking fight that had come to be agreed upon among the people as one of the fiercest since the founding of the *Vogumgata*. He had since been retired.

The fickle crowd welcomed the news, gradually lifting the mood around the arena as most of them began chanting, "Bavarus! Bavarus! Bavarus!"

A smile crept upon Emordra's face as she looked on in hope.

The announcer bowed to the chanting crowd and exited the arena as The Lead Knight paraded the jousters, or *Vogums*, around the arena to raucous applause from the people and then stopped when he came up to the base of the *Petiola*.

The people grew quiet when the knight bowed his head and then asked Emordra for permission for the games to begin.

Emordra stood up from her seat. "Argalon, shall the games begin?"

"Yeeeeessssssssssssssssssssssssssssss!" the people roared in unison.

"You've heard the people," Emordra said and the Lead Knight led eight of the *Vogums* out of the arena, leaving two, one on a black horse and the other on a brown horse. The two *Vogums* who remained in the arena rode far apart to the opposite ends of the arena, and after a trumpet blast, rode toward each other on full speed with their lances stretched in front of them.

The people roared as the *Vogums* rode toward each other. As they closed in, the *Vogum* On The Black Horse did something that no one could describe because it had been quick as the flash of lightening, and the *Vogum* on the brown horse fell off his horse to the ground.

The people roared once more, clapping frenziedly as the *Vogum* who won the battle rode around the arena waving his lance in approval and victory.

"*Vogum* of the lightening strike! *Vogum* of the lightening strike!" some of the people chanted.

"Colovan! Colovan!" others chanted, comparing the *Vogum* On The Black Horse to the legendary *Vogum* of Argalon rumored to have fell a hundred *Vogums* in the *Vogumgata* on a single day without being scarred or hit with a lance.

Soon arguments erupted among the people as to whether the *Vogum* On The Black Horse could fell Bavarus. But they did not have to wait long for their arguments to be addressed for just as the *Vogum* On The Black Horse dispatched the first opponent, he fell the remaining *Vogums* setting up an interesting finale with Bavarus who rode into the arena on a white horse to raucous chants from the crowd.

Almost everyone in attendance, including Emordra, held their breath in anticipation as Bavarus and the *Vogum* On The Black Horse rode to opposite ends of the arena, and then after the trumpet blast, ran toward each other on full speed with their lances stretched before them.

They both hit each other with their lances as they closed in, but nobody fell.

Most of the people gasped, for they knew they were being treated to a special fight, perhaps one that would go down in the legendary scrolls of jousting as a contender for the fiercest fight in the history of Argalon.

As Bavarus and the *Vogum* On The Black Horse steadied themselves on their horses and rode apart once more, an old man suddenly ran from the dugout into the arena and began shouting; the old man was the Chief Priest.

"People of Argalon, you should all be ashamed of yourselves!" the Chief Priest said. "Just yesterday, your noble ruler Queen Ailith was deposed and here you all are celebrating her demise with her traitor?"

Emordra stormed to her feet at the *Petiola*, incensed, as most of the people began booing off the Chief Priest, saying he should get out of the arena for the fight to continue; others sided with the Chief Priest.

"Seize the wretch!" Emordra thundered.

Couple of guards ran from the dugout into the arena and seized the Chief Priest.

"I say the truth, Argalon!" the Chief Priest shouted as the guards seized him and began dragging him out of the arena. "Do not let her buy you with games!"

The people became divided. Some chanted, "Live! Live! Live!" while others chanted, "Death! Death! Death!"

Within a short while, the people began fighting amongst themselves in the stands, and what looked like a promising day for Emordra soon turned into a horrific nightmare.

"Get me out of here!" Emordra ordered, seething.

Her slave attendants at the *Petiola* scurried behind her as Romelot and Gazan ushered her out of the *Vogumgata*.

Upon arriving back at the castle later, Emordra barged into the Banquet Hall and began overturning the tables of mountains of roasted duck, mashed potatoes, gravy pots and gourds of mead that had been prepared for the people for the feast after the game. As she overturned the tables, Romelot and two other guards brought the Chief Priest to her.

"You wretch!" Emordra said, trembling with hate, walked over to the Chief Priest, raised her arm and swung at his face.

The Chief Priest did not flinch. She did not hate him, he thought to himself. She hated herself for her own crooked schemes.

The slap landed across his face.

"Everything was going perfectly as planned until you showed up," Emordra said, quaking spasmodically.

"I only spoke the truth," the Chief Priest replied.

Emordra drew Romelot's sword from his side and thrust it into the Chief Priest's heart, saying, "May the truth serve you well in your grave!"

PEOPLE OF THE FOREST

"Let her go! Let her go!" Dutton shouted as he struggled ceaselessly to free himself from the pole he was bound to, his voice echoing loudly in the mountains around him with the soft rays of the setting sun caressing his face.

The creatures that had captured him and Queen Ailith earlier in the morning were chanting and circling around Queen Ailith whom they had lain naked and unconscious on an altar not too far away.

"Vuuuvuvuvum! Vuvuuuuuvum!" the creatures chanted continuously like a drone of bees as they circled the altar.

"Let her go!" Dutton continued shouting and fighting more vigorously to free himself from the pole after he caught sight of a much older-looking member of the creatures wielding a gleaming knife in its hand coming out from a neighboring cave to join the others; the creature that joined the rest seemed to be the King-creature, for the rest of the creatures filed into a straight line and bowed down in obeisance as soon as he joined them.

As they bowed, the King-creature raised his hands skyward at the altar with the knife and began chanting as if praying to a god. Every now and then, the rest of the creatures that were bowing down would raise their heads, mutter some demented-seeming phrases and bow down again; it was apparent to Dutton the creatures were about to offer Queen Ailith as a sacrifice to their god.

Fighting vigorously than ever, Dutton successfully freed his right arm and hurriedly began undoing the ropes that bound his left hand and feet. He had successfully freed his other hand when he caught sight of a thick cloud of dust rising in the near distance accompanied by the sound of hoofs; it seemed as if an army was heading toward them. But surprisingly, only three horses emerged out of the cloud of dust, galloping toward the altar on full speed.

The creatures began squealing and scrambling about in fear for their lives as the men on the horses began unleashing a storm of arrows upon them. The arrows took out most of the creatures including the king-creature; the few that survived escaped into the mountains.

Upon arriving, the men rode to the altar where Queen Ailith was still lying lifeless. One of the men, who had a large scar on the left side of his face, grabbed Queen Ailith's gown, which was lying nearby on the ground, covered her up, and tried to revive her.

Dutton, who had successfully freed himself by now, came running over to the Altar. Without even asking whom the men were, he joined the Man With The Scar in helping to revive Queen Ailith by doing mouth-to-mouth rescue breathing. Soon Queen Ailith coughed to the joy of Dutton who had been growing increasingly anxious.

"Are you all right, Your Majesty?" Dutton said as Queen Ailith regained consciousness.

"I'm fine," Queen Ailith replied and sat up, feeling a bit lightheaded. After a short while she came to herself and caught sight of the men beside Dutton. "Who are you people?"

Dutton turned to the men.

"I'm Lord Petreus," the Man With The Scar replied. "This is Volmin and Suberius," he added, pointing to the two men beside him who had quivers or arrow bags on their backs.

"We are the People of the Forest," Volmin, a lanky, slightly hunched fellow said and went on to say that Queen Ailith's father had sent them to rescue her and Dutton.

"My father?"

"Her father? It can't be. Her father has been dead since ten years," Dutton interrupted.

"He appeared to me in a dream last night saying that you were in danger and needed help," Lord Petreus replied.

Queen Ailith asked how Lord Petreus came to know her father. Lord Petreus told Queen Ailith that three decades prior her father saved his village from being overrun and annihilated by their bitterest enemies, the Bravadoes.

"Why should we believe you?" Dutton said.

"You don't have to. You only need to follow me if you want to live. Soon the Dolverines would be back in full force to avenge the deaths of their king and comrades."

"Dolverines?" Queen Ailith said, getting down from the altar and slipping into her gown.

"The creatures that captured you," Suberius said. He was a short fellow with an albino complexion.

"We need to get going Lord Petreus," Volmin interrupted.

"Thanks for saving us, but we are not going with you," Dutton said.

"We are not going to force you to go with us, but you should know that you cannot survive long on your own in this forest," Lord Petreus said.

"We *have* been surviving on our own," Dutton said.

"How well was that going for you?" Volmin said.

Queen Ailith glanced at Dutton and then back at the men and asked to have a word with Dutton. The men agreed, and Queen Ailith led Dutton by the hand about five feet away.

"We can't trust them, Your Majesty," Dutton said.

"He knew my father," Queen Ailith replied.

"Your father was a popular king."

"True, but they had no reason to come risk their lives to save us if what they are saying is false."

Dutton looked with skepticism in the direction of the men; they were conversing in low tones. "What if Emordra sent them after us?" he said.

"Then they would have killed us by now," Queen Ailith replied.

Dutton stared at Queen Ailith for a while and then reluctantly agreed; he and Queen Ailith walked back to the men.

"We shall go with you," Queen Ailith said.

"Alright, let's get going then," Lord Petreus replied and asked Queen Ailith to climb onto Volmin's horse and asked Dutton to climb onto Suberius'.

Queen Ailith obliged, but Dutton hesitated briefly before climbing onto Suberius' horse.

Afterwards, with Lord Petreus leading the way, they rode out of the mountains toward the forests, toward Visalia, home of the People of the Forest...

UNEXPECTED GUEST

It was almost dawn, and the full moon sitting in the night sky shone brightly, lighting Emordra's chamber. Emordra, who was sleeping, had just rolled over in her bed and pulled the quilt over her body when she was awakened by sudden gusts of wind blowing into her chamber. Opening her eyes sleepily, she caught sight of a hooded, silhouetted figure standing in her chamber at her bay window with lightning striking around it. Frightened, she bolted up in her bed at the sight of the apparition, the sleep clearing from her eyes immediately.

"Remember me, dear friend?" the silhouetted figure said, smiling.

A sharp pain whizzed through Emordra's side at the sound of the figure's voice. Uttering a shrill, agonizing cry, she clutched her side.

"I *did* tell you I was going to pay you a visit when you least expected," the figure said.

"Who—who are you?" Emordra replied, still clutching her side and grunting in pain.

"Have you forgotten me so soon, my dear Emordra?" the figure said with a hint of disappointment and floated toward Emordra's bed. "I am Eanna, Lady of the Elgorn River. Do you now remember?"

Emordra remembered. She had to. Six moons prior she had visited Eanna for dark powers to stifle Queen Ailith's power and topple her. Eanna had given her the powers under the agreement that she would come for her reward whenever she saw fit. And now she had come to claim that reward.

"What do you want?"

Eanna turned around, floated to the window and began staring into the moonlit night.

Still grunting and clutching her side in agony, Emordra raised her head slightly, stared at Eanna at the window and realized Eanna looked nothing like the form she had encountered six moons prior when she visited her for powers. At present, she looked formless, ethereal, like a ghost—a form that made her completely different from her snake appearance of old. "What do you want?" she asked once more, the words barely escaping her lips.

"I want your soul, Emordra," Eanna replied with her back turned.

"My soul? You can't have that," Emordra replied. "I just began my reign. Name something else."

Eanna turned sharply at the window, starring at Emordra through bloodshot eyes. After a short while she said, "In that case, I want nothing less than your sister's beating heart on a platter."

"My sister escaped, and for all I know she could be dead somewhere in the Elgorn Forest."

"How is that my problem? Find her or come the next full moon when I return for my reward and you fail to deliver, I *will* take your soul," Eanna said, and then disappeared in a cloud of smoke, leaving Emordra uttering another shrill cry and writhing about in pain in her bed.

Emordra's cry drew Romelot from outside this time around; he had been standing guard outside her chamber without hearing a thing earlier.

"Your Highness, is everything all right?" Romelot said as he came running into the chamber wielding a burning torch and saw Emordra hunched in her bed, clutching her side and whimpering. "Oh my, you are bleeding from your eyes and nose!" Romelot remarked as he got closer to the bed.

"F-fetch the physician," Emordra managed to say through her pain.

"Aye, Your Highness," Romelot replied, turned and rushed out.

He returned a short while later with a grey-haired old man wearing a satchel around his neck behind him.

"*Vigabenda lamunana vogano!* The curse of the Lady Serpent," the old man said as he approached Emordra's bed.

"H-help me...H-help me," Emordra whimpered.

"Is she going to be well?" Romelot asked anxiously.

"Maybe," the old man said, dug into the satchel around his neck with his right hand and brought out a silver cup with round pebbles. He then knelt down, placed the cup on the ground and dropped the pebbles into them. Afterwards, he reached into his raffia bag, took out a yellow leaf, added it to the pebbles in the cup and urinated on it.

Romelot looked on in disgust.

The old man then opened his arms, looked up and chanted. The potion in the cup caught up on fire. Leaving it flaming, he grabbed the cup with his hands and handed it to Emordra saying, "Drink and you shall be whole again. Drink and life and vitality shall return to your soul."

Emordra received the cup from the old man, and with Romelot still looking on in disgust, drank the potion which tasted salty and bitter in her mouth without her being burned by the fire. Afterwards, she handed the cup back to the old man who put out the blazing fire and told her to rest.

Emordra consented, and for the next two days, remained indoors, neither eating and drinking nor welcoming attendants. When she began feeling like herself again on the third day, she went out to take a walk in the castle's garden in the cool of the morning, attended by Romelot. As she took in the sights and smells of the garden along with the cool morning air, she recalled Eanna's visit and became deeply troubled. What if she could not locate Queen Ailith and Eanna came back? What would she do? She pondered. Surely, she could not fight the mighty Eanna, and so that meant she was going to lose her soul. A cold shudder ran through her body at the terrible prospect. She knew she had to do something to avert that fate, and whatever it was, very fast as the next full moon was twenty-one days away from rising. She concluded she needed a bounty hunter, but whom? Who could she send into the forbidden Elgorn Forest after Queen Ailith? She called to Romelot.

Romelot, who had been standing guard in front of a row of frangipanis not too far away, ran over and bowed down. "At your service, Your Highness."

"Rise," Emordra said, and as Romelot rose up, said, "I would like to send you on a mission."

"What would you have me do, Your Highness?"

"I would like to send you on a mission for the search and capture of Ailith."

"In the Elgorn Forest, Your Highness?" Romelot asked with a hint of trepidation in his voice. "No living soul has ever entered that forest and made it back out alive," he added.

"I know," Emordra replied. "But I *do* need someone to go after her should she still be alive, and you are the only one I can trust."

Romelot stared at Emordra for a short while and then said, "May I suggest The Snake of Aravon?"

"Who?"

"The Snake of Aravon."

"Who is he?"

"He's a fellow so fierce the ground trembles beneath his feet when he walks. With his club, he kills dragons, and with his bare hands he slays lions."

"I have never heard of him. Can you get him to me?"

"In two days, yes."

"Make haste."

"Aye, Your Highness."

THE TRIALS AND THE COMING
OF THE SNAKE

The bell had just gone off in the Great Hall of the castle when Emordra, clad in a long white gown, entered through the east door, followed by a handful of attendants.

The crowded hall quieted down as the people, who had turned out in large numbers for the trials, bowed in obeisance to Emordra while she made her way slowly to the throne pitched on a dais along with her attendants and sat down with a beaming smile on her face. This was going to be a big day, she thought to herself as she motioned for the people to rise almost immediately after taking to her seat. For the first time she was going to preside over the affairs of the people as Queen. She had waited for this moment for so long, and now that the opportunity was before her, she was going to bask in it.

The people rose up and almost immediately the hearings began.

The first case presented before Emordra involved a dispute between two sisters and an ox.

"I would like to hear your side of the story first," Emordra said, pointing to the shorter and younger of the two sisters standing before her throne.

The younger sister bowed. "Thank you, Your Highness," she said, rose and went on to explain how about a year prior she and her sister bought identical twin oxen to work their fields, and how her sister, after unfortunately losing her ox to the ongoing plague sweeping across Argalon, had switched the two oxen, making it look like the living oxen was hers.

"That's a lie, Your Highness," the older sister immediately interrupted, vehemently denying the claim made by her younger sister by stating that the living ox belonged to her and that the dead one belonged to her sister.

"Where is the ox in question?" Emordra asked.

A man dragged the ox, which had a chord around its neck, forward.

"You believe this is your ox?" Emordra asked the older sister.

"Yes, Your Majesty."

"You believe this is your ox?" Emordra asked the younger sister.

"I don't believe, Your Majesty. I *know* so."

Emordra rose from her seat, walked up to the two sisters who were standing before her throne, and stared intently at both, searching in their eyes to see if there was any hint to suggest one of them was lying; she found none. "Give me a sword," she requested.

Gazan, who was standing guard nearby, unsheathed his sword, ran over and handed it to Emordra who took the sword and ran her fingers along its edges as the people looked on expectantly, wondering what she was going to do.

"I shall divide the ox," Emordra said to the dismay of the people gathered in the hall. "Both of you will take away half," she added, walked up to the man holding the ox, and before the younger sister could plead for her ox, raised her sword and with two quick blows, severed the ox in two.

The people gathered in the hall were flabbergasted as they stared at the gory sight before them. No one in the hall could believe his or her eyes.

"What a perversion of justice," some murmured.

Before the people gathered in the hall could come to themselves, Emordra ordered the sisters to take their shares and depart. The younger sister, who refused to take any, turned and walked off in tears as the older sister gleefully grabbed the two halves and began dragging them away.

As the sisters walked away, Emordra handed the blood-splattered sword to Gazan, turned and went to resume her seat in preparation for the next case. She had originally decided to use the trials to connect with the people and win their hearts over. But now she did not care what they taught of her.

She was just about to call for the next case when Romelot entered the hall, ran over, bowed and informed her breathlessly that he had returned from his journey along with The Snake of Aravon who was waiting outside.

"Bring him in," Emordra replied.

Romelot stood up and signaled. The doorkeepers opened the double doors, and there in the tall gilded doorway to the Great Hall stood a beast.

Standing about ten feet tall, the Snake of Aravon was huge and had a disproportionately large head and torso. Thick veins rose and stood firm on his husky arms like the stocky roots of a sequoia tree. Dirty dreadlocks drooped down his head onto his thick neck which had a large scar running from it to his face. He appeared to be breathing threatening rage through his bloodshot eyes and was carrying a giant club in his hand.

"Who dares disturb my slumber," the Snake of Aravon said in a voice that sounded like a clap of thunder and pounded the ground with his club.

Terror struck trough the hearts of the people gathered in the hall as they were mesmerized by the fierce figure before them. Even Emordra quivered slightly on her throne. It was as if she was looking upon a god of a man, one who commanded immense attention.

"He should have been named the Giant of Aravon, not a snake," Emordra muttered to herself and motioned for the Snake to come in.

The first step the Snake took caused the hall to tremble; the people started shrieking and running for cover.

Emordra stood up from her throne and motioned for the Snake to stop. "Can you hear me from there?"

"Loud and clear," the Snake thundered.

"Good. We shall conduct our business from thence."

"Fair enough," the Snake replied. "What do you want to acquire my services for?"

Emordra resumed her seat. "I should warn you, firstly, that this mission is a very dangerous one and that the prized asset is protected by a fellow of much skill when it comes to sword play. No soul or creature has ever defeated him or subdued him in a clash of swords—at least not before my eyes."

The Snake scoffed. "Do I look to you a rat? Or do you think any mortal can endure the blow of my club against his or her skull? Pray tell, what is the mission?"

"The mission is my sister Ailith, my identical twin, my nemesis. She is a fugitive on the run from justice. I need you to capture her and bring her to me alive and whole in a fortnight. She was last seen entering the Elgorn Forest. Can you do that for me?"

"I shall search for her under rocks, in the mountains, in the rivers and in the markets. I promise you, I shall bring her to you alive and whole in less than a fortnight."

"Good," Emordra replied, satisfied with what she was hearing. "What do you want in return should you deliver?"

The Snake stared at Emordra's attractive figure on the throne, licked his lips, and with a smile on his face, said, "One night with you, my Lady. Only one night."

The people gathered in the hall burst forth into derisive laughter.

Emordra raised her hand, and the people quieted down. "You shall have your wish," she replied. "Now make haste."

The Snake of Aravon turned to leave. But Emordra called him back and asked how she would know were he to be unsuccessful in his quest.

The Snake stared at Emordra for a while and then reluctantly said, "If you see a Red Starling in your garden, then know that I am no more."

The Red Starling was considered a sacred and mythical bird in Argalon as it was rarely seen. When seen, however, it often portended danger for its observer.

"Alright," Emordra replied, and the Snake turned and left in search of Queen Ailith, leaving the hall rattling to his gigantic steps...

THE NIGHT OF EREBE

For the past few days, Visalia had been busy like an anthill. The men and boys went hunting daily in droves and the women and girls stayed home cleaning and cooking. Queen Ailith and Dutton, who had been well received among the People of the Forest and felt at home, joined the din. It was that time of year when the cool, crisp breeze blowing from the northeastern Desert of Arahan came to announce *Berzali*, the season of abundance. *Berzali*, which lasted ten full days, was an occasion for honoring and giving thanks to Cova, the goddess of life and fertility, who played a greater role in the lives of the People of the Forest than any other deity. Like the cool breeze blowing from the Desert of Arahan, one could feel the excitement and joy in the air as Visalia was gripped in a festival mood.

With *Berzali* now only hours away, the final preparations were underway. The men and boys went out on their final hunting spree, and the women, girls and little children gathered together in the village playground adorning and decorating themselves. Queen Ailith, who was very excited about *Berzali* as it was not celebrated in Argalon, sat with the wives and children of Lord Petreus under a giant cotton tree, asking numerous questions about *Berzali* as Lord Petreus' head wife, Mena, a slender, youthful woman, drew a crab on her back with a dye made from powdered henna, water and the juice of unripe lime. Queen Ailith had chosen the crab because she said it matched her intuitive and cautionary nature.

"The Night of Erebe? What's that?" Queen Ailith asked in response to Mena's statement that *Berzali* was to commence at midnight with The Night of Erebe.

The sun was overhead, but its rays were as weak as a straw.

In response to Queen Ailith's question, Lord Petreus' second wife, Lotus, a chubby woman sitting beside Queen Ailith, leaned in and whispered in her ear. Queen Ailith gasped, drawing laughter from Mena and Lord Petreus' other two wives, Cemas and Demis, who had an inkling of what Lotus had told Queen Ailith; the three children sitting beside them were clueless.

"And where would the children be at that time?" Queen Ailith asked.

"Asleep," Cemas replied in her soft voice.

"Right," Queen Ailith replied with a realization that her question had been silly.

"Is it true what my father said?" Cemas' daughter, Belinda, interrupted; she was no more than ten and her mother was braiding her hair.

"About what?" Mena said.

"About what happens with the women in the cave during Erebe?"

"It takes place in a cave?" Queen Ailith interrupted, her eyes lighting with surprise.

Lotus nodded to Queen Ailith and stared suspiciously at Belinda who seemed to know too much for her age. "What *exactly* did your father say happens to the women in the cave?"

"He said the goddess brings them babies in a basket."

The women laughed, for they knew what Belinda meant.

They were interrupted as the men and boys started coming back to the village. The women rose and went to welcome them. Queen Ailith rose as well and went to welcome Dutton who was dragging a dead animal behind him. She kissed Dutton on his lips upon coming up to him and hugged him; they had grown closer to each other since arriving in Vasalia.

After letting go of each other, Queen Ailith smiled a flirtatious smile and then turned around to show the crab tattoo on her back.

"It's beautiful. *You* look beautiful as always, Your Majesty," Dutton said, smiling.

"Thank you," Queen Ailith said and looked behind Dutton. "What do you have there? Bison?"

"Your favorite," Dutton replied, smiling.

Queen Ailith reached out and held Dutton's hand. "So…are you ready for The Night of Erebe?" she asked with another flirtatious smile on her face.

Dutton, who had been informed by his hunting mates about The Night of Erebe, smiled. "We'll find out tonight, won't we?"

Festooned with bandoliers of cowry shells crisscrossing her chest and breasts and with layers of straw cascading down her waist, Queen Ailith shook her hips, and moved her slender body to the right, and then to the left with her arms moving back and forth like a swimmer performing the breaststroke as the drums roared. It was the first part of Erebe, and she was dancing *Mgbadza*, the local tribal fertility dance, after being coerced by Mena and her friends. All around her the women of Visalia, also draped in straw and cowry shells, moved their bodies back and forth as well, sipping and bathing with wine from gourds they carried as torches mounted on forked pillars made from smooth logs blazed around them. Most of the men, acting as lewd clowns, engaged in exaggerated sexual horseplay around the women as they danced. Shortly after the celebration, they would all head to the caves scattered around the village for the main part of the fertility rite to commence.

Glistening with sweat and wine, Queen Ailith continued dancing. Dutton danced over from one of the drums he had been beating along with Lord Petreus and a handful of men and began dancing with her. They stood facing each other, moving their bodies left and right as they danced to the drum's voices which rose and fell in a rhythmic fashion—–accentuating their every move and step. Where were their worries now? Where were their fears? They were gone with the cool night breeze blowing about them as they danced...

Covered from head to toe with a white chalk that smelled like cinnamon, Queen Ailith was lying fully naked on a straw bed strewn with rise petals in a well-lighted cave lined with burning torches mounted on the wall...waiting. A feeling of excitement and fear coursed through her as she ruminated on the fact that any moment Dutton was going to walk into the cave to have her. She had been with Dutton for a few days now, but the fact that they were going to consummate their relationship in a fertility rite in a strange land made her feel a bit uneasy. She would have preferred to experience such intimate moment within the castle walls of Argalon, but fate had decided otherwise.

Quickly shaking off the uneasy feeling, her mind drifted to the other women of Visalia who were also lying in caves in other parts of the village. She wondered who was going to be with Mena, Cemas, Demis and Lotus considering that they were all married to Lord Petreus. Maybe Lord Petreus was going to have to hop from cave to cave through the night to have them all, she concluded and almost laughed at her repulsive thought.

She was drawn out of her thoughts when she caught sight of Dutton standing at the entrance to the cave. His body was gleaming with sweat, and instead of a robe, he had a strip of loincloth wrapped around his waist, passed between his legs and fastened in the back. She sat up in the bed, her breathing quickening as Dutton began taking slow, gentle steps toward her like a tiger on the prowl. Smiling, she was about to say something regarding his awkward movement, but decided against it, allowing her thoughts to float away on the cool midnight breeze blowing into the cave.

Within a short while Dutton was upon her. Without saying a word, he sat on the bed, looked into her eyes, reached toward her and kissed her gently on the lips; his breath smelled of the palm wine they had been drinking all evening. The palm wine was made from the palm fruit. She had been introduced to the sweet and sour yet intoxicating wine the first day they arrived in Visalia.

Rubbing Dutton's chest, she laid back on the bed as he reached in once more and started kissing her passionately, caressing his fingers along her slender neck. Shuddering with desire, her breasts pressed against Dutton's chest as his breath warmed her neck and his strong arms held her in place. She gasped and clung to Dutton, digging her fingers into his muscular back after he undid the cloth from around his waist and entered her.

"I'm happy we are together," she whispered softly as they both allowed their souls to drift into ecstasy…

THE MOURNING AFTER

Visalia was still swallowed up in sleep when the gong started going off. It was the Call of the Dead gong, a ritual that took place every other day before dawn. The gong would sound and the people of Visalia would rise from bed and gather in the central cemetery to pay homage to the dead and departed.

Queen Ailith, who was lying naked in Dutton's arms, stirred in her sleep. "Not again," she protested as predawn light trickled through cracks in the walls of the cave they were lying in onto her face.

"They do truly respect the dead," Dutton replied, waking; in fact, he had hardly slept during the night and had been on his guard watching over Queen Ailith in order to protect her should any creature barge into the cave they were in.

Queen Ailith opened her eyes. "Don't they know I'm still enjoying your roomy bosom?"

Dutton kissed her on the forehead. "We have to honor their customs," he said, lifted her head from his bosom and sat up in the bed.

"You took away all my energy last night," Queen Ailith said, smiling as she rested her head onto the bed.

"That explains all the marks on my back," Dutton replied, and jumped off the bed when Queen Ailith reached over to slap him. Laughing, Dutton picked up Queen Ailith's gown which was lying on the floor and threw it at her, saying, "Hurry up and get dressed."

"Hey, I'm still your queen, and I demand your utmost respect."

Dutton laughed and bowed his head. "Pardon my impudence, Your Majesty."

"Pardon granted," Queen Ailith replied, smiling.

Dutton reached for his loincloth from the foot of the bed and began wrapping it around his waist as Queen Ailith rose from the bed reluctantly, slipped into her gown, and afterwards, they exited the cave into the misty morning, holding hands.

Shortly after exiting the cave, they came across Mena and Lord Petreus on a narrow foot path sandwiched on both sides by bushes with the rest of the forest to their right. Exchanging greetings, Dutton and Lord Petreus conversed in low tones behind as Mena and Queen Ailith took the lead on the footpath.

"You can't stop smiling, can you?" Mena said smilingly as she and Queen Ailith walked.

"Am I?" Queen Ailith replied, a hint of shyness in her voice.

Mena nodded. "So how was the night?"

"Interesting."

"Interesting?"

"Aye, interesting," Queen Ailith replied, shocked that Mena wanted to get all the details of her intimate life. "How was yours?"

"Well, I do think the goddess brought me a basket load of babies this time," she replied and she and Queen Ailith laughed.

They were interrupted when a wolf suddenly jumped out of the forest into their path, snarling. Queen Ailith jumped back instinctively, leaving Mena, who seemed unfazed, standing before the wolf; Lord Petreus held back Dutton as he made to run over. "Mena will take care of it," he said.

"Don't panic," Mena said to Queen Ailith and then said to the wolf, "We do not seek to harm you, noble wolf. We are merely travelers who realize we have encroached on your territory. We shall give you way and you shall give us way."

The wolf snarled and disappeared back into the forest, leaving Queen Ailith flabbergasted.

"You talk to animals?" Queen Ailith said, trying to comprehend what had happened as Lord Petreus and Dutton walked over.

"Wolves," Mena replied. "A gift I received from my grandfather," she added and they began walking on.

A short while later, they veered off the foot path, rounded a group of trees and entered the cemetery where majority of the people were already gathered praying. As they made their way through the crowd, heading to the front, they heard a thunderous roar accompanied by the mention of Queen Ailith's name. The people gathered in the graveyard turned and caught sight of the towering Snake of Aravon running toward them from the west, wielding his club with the ground trembling beneath his feet. Shrieking in fear for their lives, the people disbanded, running helter-skelter and trampling one another as the Snake closed in on them and began swinging his club, smashing skulls and sending blood splattering about.

The People of the Forest had been taken by surprise as they had no weapons with them and were vulnerable.

"We have got to stop him," Dutton said, and he and Lord Petreus told Queen Ailith and Mena to stay put and ran off between the people scrambling about to the Snake. Both Dutton and Lord Petreus leapt onto the back of the Snake as they approached and began hammering the Snake's head with their fists. The Snake turned around as he tried to gain control over the situation and then reached his hand to his back, grabbed hold of Lord Petreus and sent him flying; Lord Petreus crashed into a tree not too far from Queen Ailith and Mena who both ran up to him and asked whether he was fine.

"I'll be fine," Lord Petreus said, grunting in pain.

Before Queen Ailith and Mena could help Lord Petreus onto his feet, Dutton landed beside him, letting out a pitching cry and holding his back. Turning, Mena suddenly let out a pitching cry like that of a wolf as Lord Petreus stood up to his feet.

"What are you doing?" Queen Ailith said to Mena before running over to Dutton to help him onto his feet.

Mena continued letting out the cry, and within a short while, a pack of wolves emerged from around the forest and crowded up in front of her, snarling viciously.

"Please, we need your help," Mena said to the wolves and then pointed to the Snake who was still swinging at the people scrambling about for their lives. "This giant is evil!"

Snarling, the wolves turned and began heading for the Snake. As they approached, they leapt upon the Snake who swung his club at the first one, smashing its skull. Lord Petreus, Dutton, Queen Ailith and Mena stood watching along with a handful of people as the rest of the wolves charged onto the Snake and began biting him all over his body.

Struggling to gain control of the situation, the Snake seized two wolves by their necks and sent them flying into the nearby trees. But being inundated, the Snake soon fell a mighty fall, causing the ground to quake and a couple of trees to break and smash to the ground. Before long, the Snake uttered a howl and was dead as the wolves feasted on his flesh.

By this time most of the men who had run off earlier were returning from the village with swords and bows and arrows. Volmin, who was among them, ran over to Lord Petreus, Mena, Queen Ailith and Dutton with his sword and asked whether they were fine.

"We are," Lord Petreus replied.

"Hopefully the bastard didn't kill a lot of our people," Volmin said, and he, Lord Petreus, Mena, Dutton and Queen Ailith began walking around, surveying the corpses lying about.

Within a short while, they found Lotus' corpse beside one of the graves; she had been trampled. A sunken feeling descended upon Queen Ailith and Dutton as Lord Petreus, Mena and Volmin knelt beside Lotus' corpse and began weeping. They both knew it was because of them that death had visited Visalia. Also, they knew that it was because of them that a long shadow was going to be cast on the rest of *Berzali*...

MEET ARGALON'S PROVINCIAL RULERS/GENERLAS

The hall was filled with raucous laughter. The generals seated at the table laughed as General Rubius teased General Beltus for the bleached leather sandals he was wearing.

"That's what my great, great, great, great, great grandparents wore back in the day," General Rubius said, laughing.

Dressed in sleeveless black robe with a sword worn around his waist, Rubius was a fellow of small stature, and his nose was like a thick finger poking at you when he spoke. He was general and ruler of the Province of Sud, one of the twelve provinces comprising the Kingdom of Argalon.

They were at a meeting for generals and rulers at General Grizen's castle in the Province of Marfa, the second largest province, with the Province of Aravon being the first. The meeting had been called by

Grizen to address the issues facing the Kingdom of Argalon. But for now they took to teasing each other as was their custom. There were eleven of them; Emordra should have been the twelfth, as she used to be the chief general of Argalon under Queen Ailith's reign, but she was missing.

General Beltus, a much older fellow wearing a bushy mustache resembling that of a cat's whisker, laughed from across the table and asked General Rubius whether his mother was the one who dressed him. Beltus was general and ruler of the Province of Zavala.

The other generals seated at the table burst forth into raucous laughter, some clapping and stamping their feet.

"Good one," General Oryx, a large fellow, said from beside Beltus. He was ruler of the Province of Jotan, which was nestled in the northwest corner of the kingdom.

"Good fashion, like beauty, lies in the eyes of the beholder," Pacifus interrupted with a serious look on his face. He was the oldest among them, had long gray hair, and was wearing an eye patch on his left eye. He was the General and ruler of the Province of Ella, which bordered the Province of Aravon to the west.

"That's what a person who dresses with one eye would say," General Quipps, a young fellow with blonde hair, said from beside

Grizen as the Generals stared at Pacifus who had on a lackadaisical blue robe and laughed.

Pacifus only shook his head; he was often the object of ridicule among them.

"It's enough now, Gentlemen," Grizen eventually interrupted in his guttural voice, standing up and clearing his throat. He was an imposing figure with a sturdy build and was the general and ruler of the Province of Marfa.

The laughter began dying down in the hall.

"We may have gathered here in mirth, but make no mistake our kingdom is in grave trouble," Grizen continued. "It's no secret what has happened to our beloved Queen Ailith. An imposter of a sister has deposed her. Shall we all just sit and do nothing while Emordra has her way amongst us? I say no, for when our ancestors pledged to join forces with Argalon to form the Kingdom of Argalon centuries ago, it was done in good faith and with the understanding that no decision was ever going to be made without our collective counsel."

"Right!" a lanky fellow with a lazy right eye interjected across from Grizen. That was General Vaga, ruler of the Province of Lodin, which bordered the Province of Marfa to the west.

"But Emordra engineered a coup and toppled the legitimate ruler without first consulting with us," Grizen continued.

General Beltus coughed loudly and sniffed, inviting suspicious stares in his direction.

Grizen paused and studied Beltus' face. "From your expression it appears you did know of the coup before it happened," he said.

Beltus shifted uncomfortable in his seat, looking at Grizen with an enigmatic look on his face.

"Did you know, Beltus?" Grizen asked militaristically.

"M-mostly from hearsay...you know...words on the street," Beltus stammered.

"Hearsay? Words on the streets? And yet you did nothing to prevent it?" Vaga interrupted.

"How about you Dextrus? Casein? And you, my lovely friend Rubius?" Grizen asked.

Grizen received blank stares from the generals he mentioned.

The hall that was filled with laughter moments earlier now took on a solemn air.

"Wow, I do feel I'm in the midst of traitors," Grizen said, immediately drawing his sword, and pinning it to the neck of Rubius who was sitting to his right.

Except for Pacifus, the rest of the generals stormed to their feet, each drawing his sword and pinning it to the other's neck; it was five against five.

"And you, Rubius?" Grizen said as he held firm to his sword which was still pinned to Rubius' neck.

"I could not tell you about the coup before it happened because of your loyalty to Ailith," Rubius replied.

"What did that witch Emordra promise you all, traitors?" Grizen said, staring at Beltus, Casein, Dextrus, and Akadie.

"Does it matter?" Casein, who had his sword pinned to General Vaga's neck replied. He was a fellow of moderate height and was the general and ruler of the northwestern Province of Agas.

Pacifus finally stormed to his feet. "Generals! this would not get us anywhere. Should we choose to slay one another here, this will not be the end, but the beginning of a bigger bloodbath. Besides, the problems Argalon face will still remain should we all be lying in our graves. Is that what we want? I urge you all to reconsider and lower your swords."

Pacifus looked at Grizen who was seething with contempt toward Rubius. Grizen stared back at Pacifus and then Vaga and the other four generals on his side and reluctantly lowered his sword.

Vaga, Bados, Oryx, and Quipps, the generals on Grizen's side, did likewise.

"Get out now, traitorous bastards, before I change my mind!" Grizen exploded.

Beltus, Rubius, Casein, Dextrus and Akadie sheathed their swords and scurried out of the hall like rats.

"And you, traitor Rubius," Grizen called out as Rubius and his colleagues exited the hall, "there will be blood between us the next time we lay eyes on each other!"

Rubius neither looked back nor replied. He and his colleagues only kept moving.

The hall was silent and tense after Rubius and his colleagues left. It was now apparent to Grizen and his comrades that in its two centuries of existence, for the first time Argalon was divided, and perhaps, was on the brink of civil war...

GOTHIA

The sight of a village in the near distance brought Queen Ailith and Dutton a sigh of relief. They had been riding all morning since leaving Visalia after convincing Lord Petreus that it was in everyone's best interest for them to leave as Emordra was likely to send another bounty hunter after them should she discover that the Snake was dead. The journey through the Elgorn Forest had not been merciful to them, however. They had had to battle Dolverines along the way, leaving them battered and spent. The sight of the village atop a hill ahead of them could not have come at a much needed time as the evening sky above them was ominously dark and pregnant with rain.

A series of heavy thunder claps and lightning strikes in the gloomy rain-laden sky sent Queen Ailith and Dutton spurring their horses and galloping on full speed toward the village.

A young woman suddenly came running toward them as they approached the entrance to the village; the woman seemed to be running away from something as she was repeatedly looking over her shoulder as she ran.

"Help me! Please, help me!" the woman wailed as she ran and fell in front of Queen Ailith and Dutton who halted their horses, dismounted them, ran and squatted beside the woman; she had huge boils, sores, and gray patches of mottled flesh and festering lesions all over her face and body and blood was oozing from her nostrils and eyes.

"Death," the young woman said almost in a whisper, coughing out blood. "There is death everywhere," she added and gave up the ghost, frothing at the mouth.

A feeling of horror descended upon Queen Ailith who turned her head and stared into Dutton's eyes. They both knew the signs were not good.

Yet another series of heavy thunder claps and lightning strikes sent them climbing back onto their horses and riding into the village to seek shelter.

An acrid stench of piles of dead, decaying bodies greeted them when they entered the village, which looked completely deserted. Holding their breaths while plodding through the scads of dead bodies that littered the ground like abandoned garbage with rats squealing around them, Queen Ailith and Dutton wondered what had killed the people.

"The plague," Queen Ailith suddenly said; they both knew they were in some part of the Province of Aravon. But which part?

"Never knew it was this powerful," Dutton replied as a series of lightning strikes illuminated what appeared to be a signboard ahead of them; the signboard had the word "Gothia" scribbled on it.

Another series of lightning strikes sent Queen Ailith calling Dutton's attention to a venue of vultures and two dogs feasting happily on a group of bodies in front of a nearby shed to her right. Turning his head, Dutton saw a vulture pecking out the eyes of a dead prisoner who had been locked up in the stocks, which is a restraining instrument used to lock up prisoner's hands and necks in order for them to be publicly humiliated. The sights aroused fear and disgust in him and Queen Ailith, and as they tried to plod on, strange sounds like dying people shrieking began rising around them. Queen Ailith instinctively pulled her horse closer to Dutton's, and in that moment, they heard a loud animal-like howl; the vultures flitted away and the dogs bolted, barking fiercely, and Queen Ailith caught sight of what appeared to be a silhouetted figure running between the huts.

"Did you see that?" she asked.

"What?" Dutton said.

"I think I just saw a ghost."

"I wouldn't be surprised," Dutton replied. "This place looks haunted," he added.

In that moment, the gloomy clouds burst above them, and as they made to go seek shelter, a queer thing began happening around them: the dead started to rise.

"It can't be," Queen Ailith said as she and Dutton, cantering their neighing horses, drew their swords and began slashing their way through the undead which were rising around them and pouring in from every quarter of the village.

Blood splattered about them as they hacked and chopped with every ounce of strength left within them, thunder clapping and lightning striking repeatedly above them.

Despite their efforts, the undead were not dying.

"They are not dying," Queen Ailith said, breathless as she swung at an undead.

"Chop of their heads!" Dutton replied, stepping an undead that had closed up on his horse and cutting off its head with a perfect swing of his sword; the undead exploded, sending body parts flying about: a bloody hand landed on Queen Ailith's chest. She pulled it off, threw it away and swung at another undead that had closed in on her; the undead's head went flying off its body.

"We need to get out of here," Queen Ailith said as she and Dutton spurred their horses, galloping off and swinging at the undead before them.

The undead chased after Queen Ailith and Dutton as they exited the village, panting, with the rain pouring on them horrendously…

FAIR GAME

Rubius was pacing back and forth the empty library of Castle Argalona with a frantic look on his face when Emordra walked in.

"You wanted to see me in private?" Emordra said as she entered alone with her long blue gown trailing behind her.

"Yes, yes," Rubius replied, turning to face Emordra. "He knows."

"I don't quite follow. Who knows what?"

"Grizen. He knows that I, Casein, Dextrus, Beltus and Akadie knew about your planned coup before it happened."

"Well, he was bound to find out sooner or later."

"You were supposed to take care of him right after you took power."

Emordra turned and began walking gently; Rubius followed her, waiting for an answer.

The sunlight filtering through the window shone brightly onto the spines of books and scrolls on the towering shelves beside them.

"That was the plan. But things happened that demanded my utmost attention, and I had to attend to them."

"He's threatening to kill me."

"Grizen might be a drunk but he's no fool. I would deal with him drastically should he dare lay a finger on you."

"And Argalon?"

Emordra stopped and turned to face Rubius who also stopped.

"What about Argalon?"

"Can't you see we are divided? Vaga, Bados, Oryx, Quipps, and perhaps Pacifus, are on his side."

"Calm your mind, Rubius. Argalon shall be fine," Emordra replied, adding that she was going to invite Grizen and his allies to the castle to talk things over.

"And should they refuse to come?"

"Then we might have to resort to Plan B."

Rubius stared intently into Emordra's eyes; apparently, he understood what she meant.

Grizen, Vaga, Bados, Oryx, Quipps and Pacifus were all seated in the Great Hall of the castle, engaged in conversations amongst themselves when Emordra walked in, flanked to her left and slightly behind by Rubius, Casein and Romelot and to her right by Dextrus, Beltus and Akadie.

It was a few days after Rubius' visit. Like she had promised Rubius, Emordra had invited Grizen and his allies to the castle for a meeting.

Grizen immediately stormed to his feet upon catching sight of Rubius. "Traitorous bastard! Today you die!" he shouted, drew his sword and came running.

Romelot intervened, drawing his sword and blocking Grizen's sword with his after he approached and swung at Rubius. "How dare you draw your sword before the queen?" Romelot said as his and Grizen's swords locked together.

"And what do we have here, mommas' boy?" Grizen said. "You better step aside before I chop you into pieces in his place."

"Why don't you give it a try?" Romelot replied.

Rubius, Casein, Dextrus, Bados, and Akadie drew their swords as Pacifus, Vaga and the rest of Grizen's allies ran over and intervened, asking Grizen to lower his sword; Grizen refused.

Emordra, who had been watching and seething with anger, eventually interrupted. "Enough! Enough of the farce!" she exploded, the snakes on her head beginning to writhe. "Grizen! Take your seat! Now!"

"I *will* not take orders from you," Grizen replied with his and Romelot's swords still locked together. "You are not my queen."

"You are forcing my hand, Grizen," Emordra replied. "I *will* not take insults from you."

Pacifus interrupted once more, pulling Grizen away. Afterwards, he turned to Emordra. "Forgive my friend's impetuosity, Emordra, I mean Your Highness. We came in peace."

"I have always had the utmost respect for you, Pacifus," Emordra replied. "Your graceful words have been accepted. All hard feelings shall be dispelled from the heart, and we shall now turn our attention to the chief reason for our gathering."

"Thank you, Your Highness," Pacifus replied, bowing his head briefly. Upon raising his head, he turned to the rest of the generals and said, "Generals, may we all take our seats."

Still fuming, Grizen reluctantly sheathed his sword, and he and his allies went and took their seats at the table. Rubius and his friends sheathed their swords as well and went and took their seats, including Emordra who sat at the head of the table with Romelot standing guard behind her.

Shortly after everyone was seated, Emordra cleared her throat and began addressing them. "Generals, I understand your anger, especially you, Grizen. I too would have been angry if I had been left out of a major political decision. Unfortunately, what happened, happened and we can no longer go back in time to make things right. The only thing we can do now is to move forward, that is, to forge a new alliance in the hope of steering the Kingdom of Argalon, which we all love dearly, toward a brighter, unified tomorrow."

As Emordra spoke, Grizen, still seething with rage, fixated his gave on Rubius who was sitting directly across from him at the table.

"With that said—" Emordra continued, but before she could finish the statement, the unexpected happened: Grizen stormed to his feet, drew his sword, and in a blink of an eye, leapt across the table like a praying mantis, and in a single stroke, cleanly severed Rubius' head from his body.

There was deafening silence in the hall as the generals on both sides froze in disbelief at the ghoulish sight and with questioning looks on their faces that said, "Why did he do it?"

Before Romelot could move toward Grizen who stood fuming beside Rubius' severed head with his sword dripping blood, Emordra stormed to her feet angrily, stretched her right hand and sent Grizen flying into the back of the hall with a lightning bolt; his sword flung aside, Grizen slammed into the wall and fell to the ground. Before he could stagger back to his feet, Emordra raised him into the ceiling with powers shooting from her stretched hands.

Grizen hung up the ceiling, screaming for his life.

Pacifus and Vaga stood up and began pleading with Emordra to have mercy on Grizen; Emordra would have none of it. She chanted and before they realized, Grizen exploded and his innards and body parts went flying about.

The rest of the generals looked on in horror—it was a sight they would never forget.

"Anybody else?" Emordra said, scanning the faces of the fear-stricken generals with an angry look on her face.

Not a single soul stirred or whispered a word, except Pacifus and Vaga who resumed their seats.

"Didn't think so," Emordra said, resumed her seat, and pretending as if nothing happened, said, "Now back to business..."

EGRANE

The entrance to the cave was lined with numerous skulls. Emordra watched her steps as she plod through the skulls gingerly into the impenetrably dark cave with a blazing torch in her right hand, wondering why someone would choose to live in such grim and dingy-looking place.

It was a day after her meeting with the generals. Earlier in the morning, she had come across a Red Starling in the garden of the castle. The sight of the Starling flitting about her garden had arrested her attention so much that she froze in her steps, for it reminded her of the Snake of Aravon. She knew he was dead because that was the sign he gave her before leaving in search of Queen Ailith. With the Snake whom she had pinned her hopes on dead, she knew she had to hatch out another plan before Eanna came back. It was then that she decided to pay a visit to Egrane, the Oracle of the Caves.

Emordra brushed away a shrub jutting out from the wall of the cave as she plodded her way deep into the darkness which was beginning to feel alive on her skin like a leech. Scratching her skin every now and then, she kept moving. She had hardly gone fifteen paces, however, when she stepped on a dry stick, and a rope strapped around her left leg and catapulted her into the roof of the cave like an animal caught in a trap; the torch dropped from her hand and went off, leaving her screaming for her life in the dark while hanging upside down like a roosting bat.

"Help me, Egrane! Help me!" she screamed, her voice echoing through the cave like the rumbling sounds of many waters.

There was no response.

She tried to use her powers to free herself; they were useless. It was as if her powers had melted within her and evaporated into the immense darkness about her.

Screaming and struggling, ropes that she could not see fell from opposite ends of the cave and strapped her arms, stretching her to breaking point. Assuming an upside down posture, she felt as if her arms were going to break off her body; she began screaming louder as the pain was unbearable.

Soon, whips that she could not see began lashing her all over; she wailed and wailed as she was lashed repeatedly for what seemed like an eternity. When the beating finally ceased, the ropes disappeared from around her arms and leg, sending her tumbling to the ground with a giant thud.

Bleeding severely and drunk with pain, she staggered to her feet in an attempt to run back out of the cave; it was then that the cave lighted up and what appeared to be a grim and dingy-looking cave transformed into a magnificent hall with high vaulted ceilings.

"Welcome! Welcome to the Oracle of the caves," a voice boomed.

Squinting, as the light was too bright in the hall, Emordra caught sight of a gray-haired man with long white beard sitting cross-legged on the floor; that was Egrane, her and Queen Ailith's former magic teacher at the castle when they were children. (Egrane had given up the post and retreated to the caves shortly before Emordra and Ailith's mother passed on their tenth birthday).

"Why did you torture me, Egrane?" Emordra said.

"Everyone sees and experiences different things when they come to visit me," Egrane replied. "What you saw and experienced upon entering the cave are what are within you, Emordra: you are a helpless, tortured soul filled with death and darkness."

The words stung Emordra's heart; she stared at Egrane with an uneasy silence between them.

"Come. Have a seat," Egrane eventually broke the silence and Emordra lurched over and sat across from him on the floor. "Are you badly wounded?"

Emordra nodded and Egrane raised his hands and motioned in the air as if he were drawing a circle; a big yellow leaf appeared into his hands.

"This should numb the pain," he said, handing the leaf to Emordra who took it, put it in her mouth and began chewing; the leaf tasted bitter in her mouth but caused her bleeding and pains to cease and disappear almost immediately.

"You forsook us," Emordra said, grimacing, as she continued to chew on the leaf.

"I didn't. *You* and your sister forsook me."

Emordra scoffed.

There was another moment of uneasy silence between them as they stared at each other. Egrane looked much older to Emordra than he was when he served at the castle. Back then he was young and filled with energy. She remembered when he first taught her and Queen Ailith how to cast spells at the ages of eight, and how almost immediately, she set his hair on fire and how he had chased her about saying little children should never play with fire or they would get their fingers burned. As she sat across from him, she could see him jumping about in her mind with his hair blazing. The thought brought her found memories and made her smile.

"So you've been living alone all these years?" Emordra broke the silence.

"I've been here with my friends."

"Friends? Where are they?"

Egrane clapped, and all of a sudden, a tiger, a lion, a cheetah, a snake and an orangutan emerged through the walls into the hall.

Frightened at the sight of the creatures, Emordra scooted toward Egrane.

"Don't be frightened. They won't harm you…Well, not until you give them reason to," Egrane said and then beckoned to his friends to come over.

The creatures came up, and Egrane introduced Emordra to them. The animals made a diversity of sounds in response as Emordra greeted them.

"Go on, touch them," Egrane said.

Emordra rubbed her hands on the heads of the lion, tiger, snake and cheetah and shook hands with the orangutan. "They seem friendly," she said, smiling.

"*We are friendly,*" the snake replied, startling Emordra.

"Oh, a talking snake?" she said, smiling.

Egrane smiled as well, and as he watched Emordra pet the animals, which had now made themselves comfortable beside her, asked how Queen Ailith was.

The smile immediately disappeared from Emordra's face. "I overthrew her," she replied bluntly.

Egrane shook his head. "I saw it coming, long, long time ago when you were children," he said. "The jealousy and constant quarrels between you two…I knew it was only a matter of time before it developed into a power struggle…And that was the chief reason I left the castle. Because had I stayed I would have had to choose between you and your sister."

"Do you think what I did was wrong?" Emordra said. "I mean all these years I just wanted to be queen, to experience what it felt like, but I never thought things were going to turn out this way," she added with a hint of regret in her voice.

"Well, Emordra, sometimes we want things that are not in our destiny, and whenever we try to obtain those things regardless of the costs, we only bring upon ourselves much pain and suffering."

"But how do we ever truly know what's in our destiny unless we strive to achieve something?"

"The truth is you'll never know. But let wisdom guide your choices instead of passion alone, for passion without reason is like a blind fellow walking without his cane. Sooner or later, he'll fall into a pit, one that he cannot dig himself out of."

A moment of silence engulfed them as they stared at each other; the lion yawned.

"I think I've dug myself into a pit with my passions and need your help in digging me out," Emordra broke the silence.

"Speak, my daughter."

"It has to do with Eanna."

Egrane looked taken aback by the mention of Eanna. "Lady of the Elgorn River?"

Emordra nodded.

"What happened?"

Emordra explained to Egrane about how several moons prior she had visited Eanna for dark powers to topple Queen Ailith, and how Eanna had given her the powers under the condition that she would come for her reward whenever she saw fit.

"And what's her request?" Egrane interrupted, and Emordra told him that Eanna's request was Queen Ailith's heart on a platter, but she could not deliver as Ailith had escaped earlier with Dutton and she could not locate her, meaning her soul was going to be taken instead.

"You made a bargain with the devil for your sister's heart?"

"A thing I now regret in hindsight."

"And you were going to offer your sister in the process had she not escaped?" the snake interrupted.

Emordra stared at the snake. "I had hoped that would not be an issue."

Egrane lowered his head; Emordra looked at him expectantly, hoping he would say something.

"Why didn't you come to me first?" Egrane said, raising his head.

"Would you have given me the powers to topple my sister whom you so love?"

"I love you both," Egrane replied and then said that he would help Emordra, but only if she promised she would spare Queen Ailith's life.

"I promise," Emordra said, and at that, Egrane raised his hands up and chanted; a gleaming gold knife appeared into his hand.

"Take this knife. The next time Eanna visits drive it through her heart," Egrane said, handing the knife to Emordra who took it and thanked him wholeheartedly.

"You just saved my life," Emordra said.

"And I hope your sister's," Egrane replied.

Emordra grinned and rose up to leave.

"Not yet," Egrane said, rising. "Follow me," he added and led Emordra out of the hall into a narrow corridor and then to the entrance of a dungeon.

Locked up in the dungeon was a gray-haired old man who looked just like Egrane, albeit a wilder version of him with long and disheveled hair.

"What do you see in there?" Egrane asked.

"You," Emordra replied.

"Aye, that *used* to be me—the dark side of me," Egrane replied. "That fellow in there is a cheat, a murderer, a traitor and a drunkard," he added.

"I never knew you were any of those things," Emordra said.

"Maybe you were too young to notice," Egrane replied, pausing briefly. "We are our own worst enemies, Emordra, and we all have that dark side in us in some shape or form, which, if left unshackled, will run amok and ruin our lives. It is by learning to make good choices that we keep it at bay."

Emordra nodded. "Do you think I can be redeemed after all the sins I've committed?"

Egrane grinned and then motioned in the air; a phoenix appeared in his right palm.

Emordra watched in astonishment as the phoenix flamed up, burnt, turned into ashes, and then after a short while, resurrected into a glorious phoenix and flew off.

"Like the phoenix, my daughter, life's a cycle of reincarnations, a cycle of births, deaths and rebirths," Egrane said. "As a result, it's never too late to shed your old self or die and be reborn; it's never too late for redemption," he added, reached out and touched Emordra's neck; a deep sleep befell her....

When Emordra woke, she found herself lying in her bed in her chamber. Sitting up in the bed with the waxing gibbous moonlight filtering through the window into her chamber, she was not sure the experience she had had was real or just a dream. She ran her hand across her body, but felt no marks or pain. Surprised, she got out of her bed and went and stood at the bay window. It was there that she saw the knife that Egrane had given her. Picking up the knife from the window sill with a beaming smile on her face, she knew she had just experienced the subtle yet mighty power of Egrane. Also, she knew she was now ready for the return of Eanna....

CAPTIVES

"Move! Move! Move, horseshit!" a Vandal wearing an eye patch on his right eye said, pushing Queen Ailith in the back. Queen Ailith fell onto the parched desert earth, the shackles and chains around her hands, neck, and feet pulling along three other captives behind her to the ground. The Vandal With The Eye Patch unfurled the whip he was holding and started whipping Queen Ailith and those who had fallen; the other captives staggered to their feet, but Queen Ailith remained down.

It was noon, but the sky overhead was overcast. Rain clouds hid the sun, but refused to release any rain. There was not a hint of wind in the desert and the humidity was so intense it curled Queen Ailith's hair into tiny tendrils on her forehead as she lay on the ground groaning.

It was few days after they had survived the attack of the undead in Gothia and had taken refuge in the nearby village of Vis, where they were captured by the Vandals—a band of outlaws and marauders who, in virtual rebellion against the throne, robbed and pillaged local villages and refused to pay taxes.

"Get up! Get up!" the Vandal With The Eye Patch said, kicking at Queen Ailith who crouched on the ground in the fetal position to avoid the kick; it was useless. The kick landed in her stomach. Uttering a shrill cry, she began writhing on the ground.

Dutton, who was a bit far back in the line of twenty captives, became incensed and tried to break free from his shackles. "Leave her alone! Why don't you pick on someone your size?" he shouted.

Another Vandal with a scar running the length of his face jumped down from his horse not too far from Dutton, pulled his dagger from its scabbard and walked up with a stern look on his face. "Shut up or I shall cut off your tongue!" the Vandal said, shoving the gleaming knife into Dutton's face.

"I'm not afraid of you or your dagger," Dutton replied.

The Vandal With The Scar scoffed, turned, and then suddenly turned back around and kneed Dutton in the stomach. "How do you like that, huh?" he said.

Dutton bent over, holding his stomach and grunting. After a short while he straightened up. "Mark my words. I shall kill you before sunset."

The Vandal With The Scar turned to his colleagues and began laughing, revealing rotted and missing teeth in his mouth. "Did you hear the chap? He's going to have me killed by sunset."

His colleagues laughed. "Silence him!" they shouted.

"I would believe him, if I were you!" Queen Ailith, who had staggered to her feet moments earlier, interrupted. "I've seen him slay more than ten men with nothing but his bare hands."

"I suppose the men he killed were cowards," the Vandal With The Scar replied and then suddenly lunged at Dutton with his dagger. Dutton swerved, and before the other Vandals could blink, Dutton wrapped his chain around the neck of the Vandal With The Scar and broke it. The rest of the Vandals, about seven in number, became incensed, unsheathed their swords, jumped down from their horses and came running towards Dutton. Dutton took a step back and braced himself for them.

Before the Vandals closed in on Dutton, however, they caught sight of a cloud of dust rising toward them.

"A Sand storm?" one of the Vandals said as they all halted.

Soon, about a dozen horses emerged from the dust, heading toward them on full speed.

The Vandals turned around, ran, mounted their horses and braced themselves for the approaching intruders.

"Give me a sword!" Dutton shouted, but no one listened to him.

"Give us swords!" Queen Ailith and the rest of the captives chorused as well, albeit vainly.

Soon the Intruders were upon them. Dutton, Queen Ailith and the twenty captives banded together as they watched the Vandals and the Intruders clash. At one moment, it appeared the Vandals were gaining the upper hand, but all that changed when one of the Intruders stepped The Vandal With The Eye Patch and plunged his sword into his stomach. Seeing The Vandal With The Eye Patch dead, the handful of Vandals left fled. The Intruders chased after them, but soon turned and came back when they realized they could not catch them.

"Who are you people?" one of the Intruders, a partially armored man wearing a hound's helm, asked as their horses came up to Dutton and the captives; he appeared to be the leader.

Dutton, Queen Ailith and the captives did not reply.

The Intruder With The Hound's Helm and the rest of his gang caught sight of urine running down the legs of a boy who was trembling with fear among the captives. They burst forth laughing.

"That one can't even hold his own," one of the Intruders said.

"Hey you, what's your name?" The Intruder With The Hound's Helm said, pointing to Queen Ailith.

"Does it matter who I am?" Queen Ailith replied.

"Ah, a feisty one, I see," the Intruder With The Hound's Helm replied. "I like feisty ladies," he added, cantered his horse closer, and let loose a slap across Queen Ailith's face.

Dutton tried to break free from his chains.

"Oh, I see. She has a lover who wants to fight for her," The Intruder With The Hound's Helm said and nodded to two of his men who dismounted their horses, moved swiftly, grabbed hold of Dutton, undid his shackles from those of the other captives with a set of keys they had grabbed from the corpse of The Vandal With The Eye Patch and led him about ten feet away.

Queen Ailith looked on anxiously as The Intruder With The Hound's Helm cantered his horse over to Dutton and his men shortly afterwards and began exchanging words with Dutton. At one moment, between the exchanges, The Intruder With The Hound's Helm drew and raised his sword like he was going to strike Dutton. Queen Ailith's heart skipped a beat. She was relieved when he lowered his sword, sheathed it, and his men dragged Dutton back and chained him to the rest of the captives.

"You're all valuable assets," The Intruder With The Hound's Helm said as he rode over and ordered that they get moving.

The other Intruders ran and mounted their horses, and afterwards, they all turned and began heading west, pulling the captives along with the sprawling desert stretching before them like an interminable waterway...

FACEOFF

Dawn was approaching. The full moon sitting in the cold, cloudless sky shone brightly, lighting Emordra's chamber. The torrential rainfall throughout the day had caused an unusual drop in the temperature. Emordra coiled in her bed in the fetal position, shivering and struggling to fall asleep. She had been awake all through the night, restless, and deep in thoughts. The past few days since her return from visiting Egrane had not been a particularly good one for her reign. The plague had gained momentum, spreading across the kingdom like a wild bush fire that could not be tamed. Also, news of Generals Grizen and Rubius' deaths had quickly spread and now Argalon was embroiled in civil war, started by factions from the Provinces of Marfa and Sud, the two provinces ruled by Generals Grizen and Rubius respectively. Even though she had dispatched troops to those provinces earlier in the night to put out the uprising, Emordra knew that nothing was guaranteed. She thought she should have known better when she killed Grizen, but how else could she have meted justice for Rubius' death?

She was drawn from her thoughts by the hooting of an owl at her window. Being familiar with the occult, she knew that was an ominous sign. But what sign? Her curiosity piqued, and she rolled out of the bed to go investigate the matter.

Just as she got out of the bed, however, Emordra caught sight of Eanna hovering slightly above the ground in the center of the chamber; she had entered without making a sound, very uncharacteristic for a woman who knew how to make an entrance. Emordra froze in her tracks at the sight of Eanna; she had known Eanna was going to be paying her a visit soon, but she was not expecting her—certainly not on this cold, bleak night.

"Hello there, friend," Eanna said.

Her greeting sounded irritating to Emordra's ears, and she who commanded words, was left speechless.

"Did I come too soon, dear?"

"N-n-not at all," Emordra stuttered, and then began moving toward her chest-of-drawers on the far wall where she had hid the knife Egrane had given her.

"Where do you think you are going?"

"To get your reward," Emordra replied, almost in an outburst. "Is that not what you came for?"

"Do you have it?"

"What do you think?"

Eanna stared at Emordra from the center of the room for a short while and said, "Make haste."

Emordra walked up to the chest-of-drawers and opened it with her back facing Eanna. She stood there staring at the knife in the drawer. She knew there was little room for error; she knew she had to strike Eanna in the heart with deft precision or else any mistake would cost her soul, her life.

"What are you waiting for, Emordra?" Eanna interrupted. "Make haste."

"I watched her bleed after I took the sword and plunged it into her heart. I can almost hear her dying cries in my ears now," Emordra said mournfully and turned to Eanna, leaving the knife in the drawer. "You made me kill my sister, Eanna—my only sister," she added.

"You killed your sister the very day you chose to topple her," Eanna replied. "Now make haste, and give me my reward."

"I'm afraid my heart weighs heavy with grief to the point that I cannot touch it," Emordra replied. "It would suffice should you come for it yourself."

Eanna stared at Emordra for a short while and then began floating toward her.

Emordra studied Eanna keenly as she approached, her heart pounding within her; it was as if the world had come to a complete standstill with everyone holding their breath and watching to see what would happen next.

The moment Eanna came within touching distance, Emordra turned sharply, snatched the knife from the drawer and swung at her; Eanna ducked as if she was expecting something to that effect. Emordra missed, but just before Eanna could rise back up, she kicked out her left leg which caught Eanna under the chin and sent her flying to the ground with her arms flailing. She had hardly landed on her back when Emordra pounced on her and drove the knife into her heart, pulled it out and drove it again, and again, and again, and again, five times, while screaming in a rage. Uttering shrill cries, Eanna pushed Emordra from on top of her after the fifth stab, staggered up with the knife in her chest as blood poured out from her. "You shall die, Emordra," she said almost in a faint whisper while floating backwards laboriously like a drunk trying to find her footing. "You shall die a slow and painful death," she added, stretched forth her right hand, unleashing a tiny needle which caught Emordra on the left hand, and disappeared through the window...

EMPEREOLE

"Come buy some pottery! Come buy some dough! Come buy some gold trinkets!"

Hawkers wailed about incessantly throughout the market, which was teeming with people and alive with a cacophony of sounds.

Led in chains by the Intruders, Queen Ailith, Dutton and the rest of the captives trudged between the people pressing against them as the searing midday sun beat upon their necks. As they trudged on, Queen Ailith took in the seeming disorganized sight, mesmerized and wondering where they were. She had never seen anything like this, not in Argalon where the markets were less crowded and better organized. With so many people pressing on each other, she wondered, how could you prevent someone from stealing from you? Before her thoughts could settle, she caught sight of a bare-chested boy of no more than fifteen jerking an old woman's raffia bag from her hand. The boy had turned around and began running off when the woman noticed him and started shouting in a strange tongue. All of a sudden a handful of men wielding clubs emerged from between nearby stalls and shops and began clubbing the boy to death. The people milling about the market stopped and began chanting "Kill him! Kill him! Kill the rogue!" as the men clubbed the boy to death without anybody intervening. Queen Ailith was shocked and disgusted with the sight, wondering why a boy of such age could be treated in that manner without a trial.

She was drawn out of her thoughts when an Intruder prodded her on. As she walked, she wondered where the Intruders were taking them. Turning her head, she caught sight of Dutton not too far behind her and wondered what he was thinking and how he felt regarding the chaos around them and their capture. Perhaps the chaos was the same in the markets of the Land of Sorovan where he said he was from, she thought. He had hardly mentioned anything to her about his land, and in fact, she hardly knew much about his past except that his parents were killed when he was a baby.

She was distracted from her thoughts once more when she heard people shouting. Turning her head, she caught sight of a group of people pelting the face of a man locked up in the stocks with rotten tomatoes and radishes. Poor fellow, Queen Ailith thought to herself, wondering what his crime was.

Within a short while, they were out of the market and before them stood a castle perched on a small hill. The castle was large like Castle Argalona, the nickname of the Argalonian castle, its tall turrets and towers almost concealing the azure sky stretching behind it. Guards lazily patrolled the crenellated parapet walls imbued with arrow slits on either side. A drawbridge sat atop a dry moat. The sight of the castle brought upon Queen Ailith mixed feelings as she knew that was where the Intruders were taking them.

The gate to the castle creaked and opened, dragging lazily to a halt as they approached and were led into the courtyard by the Intruders. As they entered, Queen Ailith caught sight of a naked woman being whipped by a guard wielding a cat o nine tails.

"Never disobey the order of the King again!" the guard said as he whipped the woman, who was screaming and bleeding.

Shaking her head at the horror, Queen Ailith was distracted when a large black bird swooped into the courtyard and landed to their right, not too far from where the woman was being beating. As Queen Ailith looked on, she noticed the bird transforming itself into a tall, muscular, gray-haired fellow in his mid-sixties.

The guards gathered around the courtyard including the woman who was being whipped and the Intruders bowed to the man saying, "Hail, King Vomesious."

The mention of King Vomesious' name struck terror in Queen Ailith. She knew in that moment that they were in the land of Argalon's sworn enemies, the Land of Moora.

Without acknowledging the people, King Vomesious turned his head and stared in the direction of Queen Ailith and the captives, and then walked off and entered the castle.

The Intruder With The Hound's Helm ordered Queen Ailith and the captives to line up shortly after King Vomesious left. As they lined up, a large fellow clad in a stained lackadaisical blue robe emerged out of the castle and grinned at them, revealing rotted, missing teeth.

"Welcome to Empereole, the capital of the great Land of Moora, and to Empereole Castle, your new home," the fellow said and introduced himself as Sir Bascus Quix, the herald for the castle.

Queen Ailith stared at Sir Bascus Quix with disgust as he motioned to the Intruders to undo their chains and shackles. Sir Manus Drescrux, her herald at Castle Argalona, was better groomed and had clean teeth, Queen Ailith thought to herself.

"Here, you shall do as you are told, and serve our king with honor and grace," Sir Bascus Quix said as the Intruders undid the shackles and chains from the captives and then clapped: a group of servant girls adorned in short see-through dresses leaving nothing to the imagination emerged out of the castle as if it was regurgitating them.

"Lead them to the baths and get them ready for service to the king," Sir Bascus Quix ordered.

The servant girls led Queen Ailith and the rest of the other female captives away, leaving Dutton, the male captives, Sir Bascus Quix and the Intruders.

Queen Ailith turned and looked over her shoulder at Dutton; she noticed Sir Bascus Quix kneeling down in front of him as she walked into the castle along with the women captives, wondering what they were going to do with him and the rest of the male captives...

REVELATION I

Standing at the bay window and staring out thoughtfully at the crowded and dusty streets of Empereole under the late evening sky, King Vomesious did not turn around when Dutton entered his sprawling chamber.

"Uncle?" Dutton said as he walked into the chamber in a red sleeveless robe and stood in the center.

"What took you so long?" King Vomesious replied in a guttural voice with his back still turned to Dutton; he was clad in a long white robe with a black velvet frock draped over his shoulder.

"I had to be thorough; I had to woo them and buy their trusts."

"Fifteen years, was it? That's how long it took you to win their trusts?"

"It was very difficult than it appeared."

A moment of silence swept through the chamber.

King Vomesious suddenly began clapping, breaking the silence. "Congratulations," he said, turned and walked up to Dutton with a beaming smile on his face. "Your thorough work now has Argalon in a vulnerable state, and a fresh intelligence just coming in says their kingdom has degenerated into civil war. That is exactly where we want them before we strike and make them history."

Dutton grinned.

"I'm proud of you," King Vomesious said, placing his right hand on Dutton's shoulder, "and I know your father and mother would have been proud of you too were they alive."

Dutton took in a deep breath on the mention of his parents. "What about Queen Ailith?" he said exhaling as King Vomesious let go of his shoulder.

"What about her?"

"Unbeknownst to her, I captured her and brought her here. But she's innocent."

King Vomesious scoffed, turned and walked back slowly to the bay window. "She has charmed you, hasn't she?" he said with his back turned. "I warned you about women, didn't I?"

Dutton did not respond.

"'Those capricious creatures live in a deluded world of their own; they are out of touch with reality, and as such, are weak points to every man's heart. A true man, should he ever succeed in his quest, should learn to fortify his heart against their whims…' those were the exact words I spoke to you before you left for Argalon fifteen years ago," King Vomesious said with his back still turned to Dutton. "But you failed," he added, shook his head, turned and walked up slowly to the adjacent wall where a sheathed sword hung.

Dutton swallowed a gulp of spit and tensed as King Vomesious unsheathed the gleaming blade and ran his fingers along its edges.

"I cannot let a weak link exist to distract us from our cause," King Vomesious said.

"What do you mean? Are you going to kill me?"

"No," King Vomesious replied. "Her."

"Y-you don't have to, Uncle," Dutton replied. "We can use her as leverage along the way. She commands the hearts of her people, and they love her dearly and would do anything for her."

They were interrupted by a loud knock on the door, and Queen Ailith, wearing a sultry short blue dress, walked in with a tray bearing a gold cup.

Dutton took in a deep breath at the sight of her.

Queen Ailith glanced in the direction of Dutton and then curtseyed to King Vomesious. "I was asked to bring this to you, Sire."

"And you are?" King Vomesious asked, still toying with his blade. He did not recognize her.

"Lyra. Her name is Lyra," Dutton interrupted.

Queen Ailith looked at Dutton with a questioning look on her face; Dutton gave her a stern look. "I'm Lyra," she said.

King Vomesious stared at Queen Ailith and then at Dutton suspiciously. "Thank you, Lyra," he eventually said.

Queen Ailith placed the tray on a nearby table, curtseyed and exited the chamber.

"Can I take my leave now, Uncle?" Dutton said as soon as Queen Ailith walked out.

King Vomesious nodded and said, "Don't do anything stupid, Dutton."

Dutton stared at King Vomesious briefly, turned, and was about to walk out hastily, when King Vomesious called him back.

"Just out of curiosity…the plague, how deadly and effective has it been in Argalon?" King Vomesious said.

"*You* brought that pernicious plague on Argalon?" Dutton asked, with an astonished look on his face.

"What? Think about it. It was a brilliant tactical move: I instigate a deadly and unstoppable plague upon Argalon through the help of the mighty sorceress Neela, Queen Ailith loses her popularity among her people because she cannot stop the plague, her power-hungry sister Emordra initiates a coup, splitting Argalon into factions, which then leads to civil war and leave them vulnerable to attack and conquer by us. What better plan could there be? Besides, you were taking too long in Argalon, and I was not sure whether you had reneged on the previous plan so I had to act," King Vomesious said, and added that in the game of war, you always have to stay one step ahead of your enemy.

Dutton gave a fake grin. "You never cease to amaze me," he said, turned and exited the chamber hastily.

As he reached outside, he caught sight of Queen Ailith in the long marble-lined corridor. He ran up to her, grabbed her by the arm and pulled her into an adjacent corridor.

"Lyra? What was that about?" Queen Ailith said, confused by Dutton's erratic behavior.

"I need to tell you something," Dutton said in a hushed voice, peeking into the hallway to see whether someone was coming.

"I also *do* need to tell you something," Queen Ailith replied, reached for Dutton's hand and placed it on her stomach. "Do you feel it?" she said, smiling.

Dutton is confused. "Feel what?"

"Don't you feel it?"

"Listen, Ailith I—"

"I'm with child, Dutton, and you are going to be a father," Queen Ailith said excitedly.

"Y-y-you w-what?" Dutton stuttered. "Heavens, what have I done?" he added, placing his hands on his head and wearing an anguished expression as if a dagger had been driven through his heart.

Queen Ailith was shocked and disappointed at Dutton's expression. "I thought you would be happy," she said.

"I-I am, but—"

They were interrupted when a guard came walking down the corridor.

"Your Highness," the guard said and bowed to Dutton as he approached.

Dutton acknowledged the guard, and the guard rose and left.

"W-Why did he call you 'highness' and bowed to you?" Queen Ailith asked, confused.

"This is what I wish to discuss. I'm not who you think I am, Ailith."

Queen Ailith scoffed. "What do you mean? You are Dutton, the warrior from the Land of Sorovan."

"I *am* Dutton, but I'm *not* from the Land of Sorovan," Dutton replied. "I'm from *this* land, the Land of Moora. I'm the Prince and King Vomesious is my uncle, my mentor and my adopted father."

Queen Ailith chuckled nervously. "Why are you saying this? Is this some kind of joke?"

"I do mean it, Ailith. You are in danger…Argalon is in danger… I--I was sent to destabilize Argalon so my uncle can conquer it."

Queen Ailith could not believe what she was hearing; a weird feeling came upon her, and the ground felt strange beneath her feet like it was caving in. She could not believe the man who had served her father and her with honor since the beginning of her reign and risked his life to rescue her from her sister Emordra could be an undercover agent. "Is it true…all what you are saying?" she asked almost at a loss for words.

"I'm afraid it is so, Ailith," Dutton replied, lowering his head in shame.

"So all the while we were on the run, I was your prisoner?"

Dutton nodded.

Queen Ailith scoffed in disbelief. "How could I have allowed myself to be blinded?" she said, recoiling as tears began rolling down her face. "W-why D-Dutton? Why? I--I loved and trusted you. And Argalon loved you. How could you do this to us?" she added as she wept.

Dutton reached in to hold her.

"Don't touch me!" Queen Ailith exploded, pushed Dutton away and suddenly took off running down the hallway.

"Ailith!" Dutton called out as he chased after her, the gap widening between them.

Queen Ailith did not look back; she only kept running, heading out of the castle as Dutton chased after her.

By the time Dutton exited the castle into the courtyard, he caught sight of Queen Ailith jumping onto a brown horse and speeding off toward the castle gate. The guards manning the gate drew their swords as Queen Ailith approached.

Dutton halted. "Let her go!" he commanded, panting.

"But, Your Highness—" one of the guards protested.

"I said let her go!"

The guards reluctantly opened the gate for Queen Ailith, who, breathless, turned and stared back at Dutton with tears streaming down her face profusely.

Dutton stared back at her, panting.

After a short while, Queen Ailith turned and spurred her horse, which sped off through the gates...

REVELATION II

It was shortly after Queen Ailith left. Dutton stood on the edge of the towering parapet in the back of Empereole Castle, looking down the craggy slopes of the hill the castle rested on. The strong winds blowing in the twilight sky hit him hard, almost pushing him over. He quickly steadied himself, and for the first time, the weight of what he was about to do crossed his mind. For a moment, he who had been through many battles and survived, felt death closer and real than ever. He knew he had been stupid to have allowed himself to fall for Queen Ailith during the process of him hatching his plan to life. But who could have resisted such a beauty? He pondered. He had felt a strong current of desire rising deep within his soul the first day he laid eyes on her in Castle Argalona. And ever since, through all those years he was laboring secretly to bring his plans to fruition, he had been hooked to her, although he had to labor tirelessly to veil his true feelings toward her until recently when Emordra overthrew her. The winds shook him again, jolting him from his thoughts. He steadied himself once more, and after a brief moment, allowed his thoughts to trail again: would suicide truly save him from his shame? He wondered. No, it would not, he concluded. All it would do was make him leave a legacy of deceit and betrayal. But he was an honest man, and would love for people to remember him as such. He must stop being a coward and go after Queen Ailith in order to mend things; he must ride back to Argalon to redeem himself, and of course, regain his queen, his love, should she be willing to forgive him.

"What are you doing, Highness?" a voice echoed behind Dutton, jolting him from his thoughts.

Turning, Dutton caught sight of Sir Bascus Quix. Ignoring him and holding onto his sheathed sword on his side, he jumped down from the parapet.

Sir Bascus Quix bowed his head briefly, raised it and said, "So is it true what they say about Castle Argalona?"

"Look, I'm in no mood for petty talk," Dutton replied impatiently and walked past Sir Bascus Quix.

"Pray tell, is it true that Castle Argalona sits on a gold mine?"

Dutton scoffed, stopped, turned and said, "Where did you hear that from?"

Sir Bascus Quix is surprised. "You don't know the prophecy?"

"What prophecy?"

"It has long been known among us that Castle Argalona sits on a gold mine of untold riches, and it has long been foretold that a great ruler would rise from among us who would conquer Argalon and gain access to the mine within which there lies the Philosopher's Stone which grants immortality to its holder."

"Are you down with wine again, Bascus?"

"Do I look like I am?"

Dutton stared at him. "How come I never heard of this?"

"Perhaps…because you read little, Your Highness…no offense," Sir Bascus Quix replied and asked Dutton to follow him if he did not believe him.

"Where to?"

"The library."

Caressing the handle of his sheathed sword on his side, Dutton stood raging within with numerous thoughts swirling in his mind as he watched Sir Bascus Quix flip through several pages of dusty books on a counter while wielding a burning torch in his left hand. He could not believe what Sir Bascus Quix had told him. King Vomesious had sent him to destabilize Argalon only because of some deluded dream about immortality? He was under the impression he had been sent to destabilize Argalon in order to create an opportunity for them to conquer it and exact revenge for the murder of his parents. What he did not know was that it was King Vomesious who actually killed his parents in an ambush on a cold winter evening on their way back from a trip to Argalon after accepting an invitation from King Debusis, the father of Queen Ailith and Emordra. That was forty years prior, and back then, Argalon and Moora were allies...and Dutton was a baby. The incident involving the deaths of Dutton's parents had brought both Argalon and Moora, ruled by King Vomesious who had assumed the throne, onto the cusp of war, one that was only averted after Kings Lodes and Crestus of the Lands of Sorovan and Varanasi respectively intervened by allying their forces with Argalon, making Argalon a mightier force than it already was.

"There!" Sir Bascus Quix suddenly said, pounding his right fist into the book opened before him.

Drawn from his thoughts, Dutton craned.

"...And there in the Cova Mountain, beneath Castle Argalona sits a gold mine," Sir Bascus Quix began reading, "containing the Philosopher's Stone which would grant immortality to its bearer, an individual who, through his immortality, would help bring back the glorious and powerful days of Moora's past..."

"It can't be," Dutton said, and just as he turned to head out of the library angrily, about five guards stormed in, wielding drawn swords and shields.

"You are under arrest, Prince Dutton, for aiding and abetting the escape of a valued prisoner," the Lead Guard said.

"Step aside. My quarrel is not with any of you…unless you want to involve yourselves," Dutton said, drawing his sword.

The Lead Guard stared at Dutton, and then nodded to his guards who immediately charged at Dutton. Dutton blocked off the first guard's attack, swung around, plunged his sword into the next guard's stomach, pulled his sword out, stepped the third guard and slit his throat, and within a short while all the guards were lying dead on the ground, excluding the Lead Guard.

Sir Bascus Quix stared in astonishment as Dutton uttered a shrill cry, leapt toward the Lead Guard, and with a single clean stroke sent his head flying off his body. Afterwards, Dutton turned and stared at Sir Bascus Quix who froze at the sight before him and then hurried out of the library, heading for King Vomesious' study.

The two guards standing guard at the entrance to King Vomesious' study drew their swords and swung at Dutton as he approached them. Dutton dodged the blows, stepped the guard to his left, and plunged his sword into the throat of the guard to his right. The guard to his left came rushing and swung at Dutton once more; Dutton bent down, plunged his sword into the foot of the guard, and as the guard uttered a shrill cry, Dutton rose up and broke his neck. Afterwards, he pulled his sword from the guard's foot and barged into the study where King Vomesious was sitting studying a map on a scroll with a blazing torch beside him.

King Vomesious lifted his head from the map he was reading as Dutton barged in, and with a mocking grin on his face, said, "I suppose I trained you well because it takes an exceptional swordsman to go through my guards with such ease and alacrity."

"You lied to me," Dutton said, trembling with hate as he pointed his blood-splattered sword at King Vomesious who looked unfazed.

"About?" King Vomesious replied.

"Don't pretend as if you know not what I mean. You orchestrated the downfall of Argalon because of some centuries-old prophecy about a gold mine and a Philosopher's Stone?"

King Vomesious rose to his feet from behind the table he was sitting at. "Fact: *we* both orchestrated the downfall of Argalon. Secondly, you are the liar here, Dutton, because for fifteen good years you lived a false identity in Argalon. And besides, I never lied to you. I just never told you about the prophecy."

"What's the difference?" Dutton replied. "I was under the impression everything was done mainly for us to avenge the deaths of my parents."

They were interrupted as a group of guards barged into the chamber and began heading for Dutton.

King Vomesious motioned to the guards to stop. "That's still the goal."

"I have my doubts, Vomesious. I'm now beginning to wonder about what all you are yet to tell me."

King Vomesious scoffed. "You know everything now."

Dutton stared at King Vomesious. "Debusis, the former king of Argalon, did not kill my parents, did he?"

"Why would you say that?"

"Did he or did he not?!"

King Vomesious stared at Dutton for a short while and with a grin on his face said, "We mortals are but shadows and dust. As such, it's in our best interest to seek immortality while we yet live and play out the petty days of our lives under the tyranny and fear of all-conquering and immortal Death whose indiscriminate sickle falls on both the just and the evil, both the noble and the plebian."

"You insane bastard! *You* killed my parents," Dutton said, feeling at once betrayed and a betrayer, like a thief swindled by another thief.

Without hesitation, he flung his sword at King Vomesious. But before Dutton realized, King Vomesious had disappeared from behind the table and was now standing on his far right beside a shelf. "You've increased your powers, you deceptive whore?" Dutton said, stunned and angry.

King Vomesious chuckled. "It's only the powerful and deceptive who survive and win in the game of thrones."

Screaming at the top of his lungs, Dutton turned and charged toward King Vomesious.

King Vomesious stretched forth his right hand and sent Dutton flying into the opposite wall with a lightning bolt. Dutton crashed into the wall, and before he staggered to his feet, the guards who had barged into the study earlier ran over and seized him.

"Let go off me! Let go off me!" Dutton said as he struggled ceaselessly to free himself.

"I see your father's weakness all in your eyes," King Vomesious said as Dutton continued screaming, spewing profanities, and struggling to free himself from the grasp of the guards. "I thought I could wean you from that weakness by taking you under my wings, but I guess the apple never really falls far from the tree, does it?" he added and motioned to the guards to take Dutton away.

"I will have my vengeance, Vomesious! I *will* have my vengeance!" Dutton shouted, struggling to free himself as the guards took him away…

ACT II: AFTER THINGS FALL APART
(LONG LIVE ARGALON)

GOADED

"Go! Go! Go!" Queen Ailith shouted as she spurred her horse furiously, her crossbow aimed in front of her; the bison was in sight now and she was closing in on it fast as the late evening sun filtering through the tree canopies shone brightly around her.

"Don't let it escape, Ailith!" she heard unidentified voices shouting from the other side of the forest.

As she made to shoot, beads of sweat cascaded down her forehead into her eyes, creating a tingling, burning sensation. Reaching to wipe the sweat from her eyes, the horse suddenly halted, and neighing, raised its front legs and threw her down. "Bullocks!" she said as she tumbled into a pile of dry leaves, her crossbow flung from her hand.

Wiping the sweat from her eyes with the back of her hand and staggering back up, she suddenly found herself engulfed in an immense darkness with the sun nowhere in the sky. Turning around, she noticed her horse was nowhere in sight as well. Startled, she began calling for help, her voice echoing through the dark forest which was beginning to come alive with weird sounds.

No one answered to her call.

Growing increasingly afraid, Queen Ailith turned to run, and in that moment, caught sight of a hooded female cloaked in white beckoning her over from an undergrowth a few feet away. She knew she was staring at a ghost, but for a moment, she thought her eyes were deceiving her. She rubbed her hands over her face to be sure.

The figure was still there.

"Who are you?" Queen Ailith eventually asked, her voice trembling.

The figure did not respond, but only kept beckoning her over.

"Can you get me back home?" Queen Ailith asked.

"Only after you come," the figure eventually replied.

Hesitating and shuddering with fear, Queen Ailith began taking slow, gentle steps toward the figure as the dry leaves littering the forest floor rustled beneath her feet, creating an eerie and haunting atmosphere. The figure disappeared as she approached the undergrowth, walked through and found herself standing in front of what looked like a giant scroll hanging in front of her with images moving on it. Queen Ailith recognized the images on the "scroll":

they depicted Castle Argalona along with the rest of the Argalonian kingdom cast under a midday sky. Soon, a blanket of dark rain clouds engulfed Argalon accompanied by thunder and lightning, and what appeared to be Emordra's face appeared in the darkness; Emordra was laughing hysterically. Soon the clouds began raining blood, and within a short while, the scroll went black!

Queen Ailith stared wide-eyed at the scroll hoping it would change but it did not. "Oh, my! What a terrible fate," she uttered in astonishment.

"The fate of Argalon depends on your fast return," a voice interrupted.

Startled, Queen Ailith turned to her left and caught sight of the cloaked female standing beside her. "But my sister…" she said, her voice trailing.

The cloaked figure motioned for her to look at the scroll once more. Queen Ailith turned. The image of Emordra appeared on the scroll. Propped up in a bed and surrounded by a handful of physicians, Emordra's face was deathly pale, almost ghostlike, and she was bloated and oozing pus from her body, which was covered with festering lesions.

"Oh, no, what happened to my sister?" Queen Ailith said, stunned.

"She's dying," the figure replied.

Queen Ailith turned and stared at the figure. "How do I know what you're saying is true?"

"You're free to choose to believe my message, but you, and more precisely Argalon, shall not be free from the consequences of your choice," the figure said and then suddenly disappeared leaving Queen Ailith disoriented...

When Queen Ailith came to herself, she found herself lying in a river of sand in the scorching desert. It was a few days after her escape from the Land of Moora upon learning of Dutton and King Vomesious' conspiracy. Opening her eyes sleepily, she caught sight of her horse beside her. It was then that it occurred to her that she had been dreaming. Dragging herself lifelessly from the desert sands, the image of Argalon being obliterated under Emordra's reign resurfaced in her mind like she had seen in her dream. "I can't let that happen. I can't," she muttered to herself, and then welling with a sudden gush of strength, ran, mounted her horse, spurred it, and began riding toward Argalon on full speed...

JAILBREAK

"Behold the former Prince of Moora who ceded his throne for the petty breasts of an Argalonian whore!" one of the guards guarding Dutton in the dungeon said and swung at him as the other two guards beside him burst forth into derisive laughter.

The blow landed on Dutton's jaw. Uttering a shrill cry, Dutton tried to fight back, but the chains binding his hands would not let him as he hung limply from the ceiling with his bare chest and back covered in welts and blood.

That had been his lot—one of torture and abuse—since he was arrested and jailed after learning that King Vomesious was the one who killed his parents.

"If you truly wanted a tasty lady, you should have asked, and I would have given you my sister," another one of the guards said, and his comrades laughed.

Dutton spat in his face; the guard slapped him across his face and punched him in the nose. Dutton uttered another shrill cry as blood ran down his nose. The third guard raised his hand to swing at Dutton, and in that moment, he was caught in the throat by a dagger. Lifting his head, Dutton caught sight of Sir Bascus Quix standing at the entrance to the dungeon with a sword in his hand. Taken by surprise, the other two guards turned, unsheathed their swords and began running toward Sir Bascus Quix who braced himself for them.

The first guard swung at Sir Bascus Quix as he came close. Sir Bascus Quix blocked his charge and stepped the second guard in his chest, sending him to the ground. Before the second guard could rise back up, Sir Bascus Quix flung the sword from the first guard's hand and thrust his blade into his throat. Incensed, the second guard ran with his raised sword and swung at Sir Bascus Quix who bent down, swept his legs from under him, and in a single stroke, sent his head flying off.

"I never knew you had such deft skills with the sword," Dutton said as Sir Bascus Quix ran over to him.

"*Camouflage*," he said, adding that when you live under a tyrant, it's always necessary to blend in and make the tyrant feel you are incapable of many things in order to save your head.

"Why are you helping me?" Dutton said as Sir Bascus Quix reached for the keys on one of the dead guard's corpse and began undoing the chains from his arms.

"We do not have much time for explanation of motives," Sir Bascus Quix replied.

Dutton stared at him. "How do I know you are not leading me into a trap? How can I trust you?"

Sir Bascus Quix stared back at Dutton. "Many years ago, before you were born, my father served your father as one of his chief counselors, but Vomesious, being jealous that your father always took my father's counsel over his, framed him and had him killed," he said, adding that all the years he served in the castle, he had been waiting for the opportunity to get his vengeance, but had been unsuccessful, and that through Dutton, he saw the chance to get that vengeance.

"I'm sorry."

"Don't feel sorry for me," Sir Bascus Quix replied, handed Dutton his sword, reached for one of the dead guard's sword from the floor and asked him to follow him. Dutton consented, and he and Sir Bascus Quix ran out of the dungeon into a corridor.

The corridor was clear and there was no sign of a single guard around. They had just rounded that corridor into another sprawling corridor, however, when they heard a wild laugh, and Dutton felt a sharp sting on his left arm and noticed blood running down his arm. "What the bloody hell was that?" he said and caught sight of a shadow circling around him and Sir Bascus Quix.

"Don't look at it or you'll turn into a tree," Sir Bascus Quix said, pulled Dutton close, and with their eyes down, said, what they had encountered was called The Shadow, which was the immortal guardian of the dungeon of Empereole Castle.

"The Shadow?" Dutton asked and screamed as he felt another sharp pain on his left arm. "How come I never heard of it while I was here?"

"It's because you read very little—again no offense."

"How do we kill it?"

"We can't. It has no weak point."

"Everything does," Dutton said, and then suddenly began running around the corridor to Sir Bascus Quix's surprise.

Dutton dove to the ground and rolled over when The Shadow swung at him. The Shadow missed, and with its image projected on the coarse wall, Dutton, having noticed The Shadow's image through his peripheral vision, flung his sword; The Shadow uttered a pitching howl and a green fluid began trickling down the wall as the tip end of Dutton's sword struck the wall. Sir Bascus Quix, who had tried to call Dutton back earlier, heard the howl, and looking through the corner of his eye, flung his sword at the wall as well; the sword pierced The Shadow's image on the wall. Uttering another shrill cry, The Shadow disappeared.

"I told you everything had a weak point," Dutton said, rising from the ground. "Not everything can be found in scrolls, you know," he added.

Sir Bascus Quix laughed, and just as he took a step toward Dutton, a dagger flew in and caught him in the back.

Surprised, Dutton turned and caught sight of a guard walking into the corridor. Incensed, he took off running toward the guard empty-handed. The guard swung at Dutton with his sword as he approached; Dutton dodged the blow, swept the guard's legs from under him, sat on top of him and began punching his face repeatedly until the guard died with his face covered in blood. Afterwards, panting, he rose up, walked back and knelt beside Sir Bascus Quix on the ground.

"P-promise me that you will get vengeance for your father and my father," Sir Bascus Quix said.

With a tear streaming down his face, Dutton nodded and Sir Bascus Quix gave up the ghost...

REUNION

"Let go of me! Let go of me!" Queen Ailith screamed, struggling to free herself as Romelot and Gazan pulled her by chains into Emordra's chamber.

Emordra, who was propped up in her bed and surrounded by a handful of physicians along with Generals Pacifus and Beltus, turned her head upon hearing Queen Ailith's voice. Like Queen Ailith had seen in her dream, Emordra's face was deathly pale, almost ghostlike and she was bloated and oozing pus from her body which was covered in festering lesions—a result of her fight with Eanna.

"We found her outside the castle, Your Highness," Romelot said.

"I came on my own," Queen Ailith retorted, staring at Emordra who looked as if she was barely breathing on the bed.

Emordra, who was surprised to see Queen Ailith, ordered Romelot and Gazan to release her—to Queen Ailith and everyone's surprise.

"Your Highness?" Romelot said.

"Release her," Emordra replied in a faint whisper.

"But—"

"I said release her!" Emordra exploded and began coughing intensely.

One of the physicians dabbed her forehead with a cloth and offered her ale from her cup. Emordra refused the ale and watched as Romelot and Gazan undid the chains from around Queen Ailith's wrists and foot.

"Leave us…all of you," Emordra said after Romelot and Gazan were done.

"But Your Highness, you grow weak and need us around," a physician said.

"Leave us," Emordra repeated.

The physicians exited the chamber together with Generals Pacifus and Beltus, both of whom bowed their heads to Queen Ailith briefly before leaving the chamber; Romelot and Gazan also followed.

Queen Ailith immediately ran over to the bed after everyone exited the chamber and hugged Emordra.

They clung to each other with tears streaming down their faces.

"Is it the plague?" Queen Ailith asked after they let go of each other a short while later and sat at the edge of the bed, wiping her face with the heel of her right hand.

Emordra shook her head. "It's a long story," she said, and a moment of silence swept between them as they stared at each other. "You have a lot of courage coming back here knowing I'm seeking your life," Emordra broke the silence.

"It's the survival of Argalon that brings me back," Queen Ailith replied. "We're not each other's enemy, sister. Dutton and King Vomesious of Moora are," she added.

"What do you mean?" Emordra asked.

"Dutton is the Prince of Moora."

Emordra scoffed. "Dutton a Prince?"

Queen Ailith nodded and said, "He was sent on a mission to destabilize Argalon, leaving us vulnerable to attack and conquer. We were only the pieces he manipulated on the game board of his master plan."

"I always suspected something cunning about him…" Emordra's voice trailed as another moment of silence engulfed them. "Forgive me, sister, for all the sins I committed against you and Argalon," Emordra broke the silence once again.

"You did no wrong, Emordra. We both made choices we believed right in our hearts while being blindsided. Our focus now should turn to saving Argalon."

"My heart yearns to right the wrongs of my past, sister, but my body is weak," Emordra said. "Death has a way of conquering and softening us all," she added, reached for the gold scepter at the head of the bed and handed it to Queen Ailith.

Queen Ailith declined to take the scepter. "I never came back for the throne, sister, but to help save Argalon."

"If you *truly* came back to save Argalon, you'll take this," Emordra replied. "You were always Argalon's legitimate ruler."

Queen Ailith starred into Emordra's eyes for a short while and then reluctantly accepted the scepter.

"I'm glad you came back, Ailith."

"Did I ever tell you that you had a good heart?"

Emordra scoffed, leaned forward and kissed Queen Ailith on the cheek. "I have something else for you."

"What?"

Emordra asked Queen Ailith to look in the last drawer of her chest of drawers. Queen Ailith stared at Emordra, placed the scepter on the bed, rose up, walked up to the chest of drawers on the opposite end of the bed and opened the bottom drawer. In the drawer she found a bundle of falcon feathers tied up with a piece of red cloth.

Queen Ailith grabbed the feathers and raised it. "Is this what you have for me?"

Emordra nodded.

"What is it?"

"Untie it."

Queen Ailith looked at Emordra questioningly and untied the cloth; a bolt of lightning shot into her. "Whoa!" Queen Ailith said, dropping the feathers as she staggered backwards due to the force.

Emordra chuckled.

Queen Ailith noticed something different about herself; she felt a sense of renewed energy as if her powers were back. Stretching forth her hands suddenly, she commanded the chest of drawers to change into a bowl; the chest of drawers changed into a bowl. Excited, she commanded the bowl to change into a sword; it did. "I've got my powers back!" she said with a big smile on her face.

Emordra smiled.

"So *you* took my powers, huh?" Queen Ailith asked.

"What? Did you expect me to have you strong and powerful before I came to depose you?" Emordra said, adding that it was Eanna who bound up Ailith's powers when she had gone to see her for powers.

Queen Ailith shook her head. "You never cease to amaze me, Emordra."

Emordra smiled. "Can you still see into the future?"

"I don't know," Queen Ailith replied. "Let me see…" she added, closing her eyes.

"What do you see for my future and Argalon?"

"Nothing," Queen Ailith replied, opening her eyes. "I don't think I got all my powers back," she added.

"I'm sorry," Emordra said.

"It's fine," Queen Ailith replied, walked up to the bed and hugged Emordra. "To new beginnings."

"To new beginnings," Emordra replied, clinging to Queen Ailith…

THE ELGORN FOREST…AGAIN

The Elgorn Forest, which was bathed in the radiance of the late evening sun, loomed slightly ahead of and below them.

"Hang on, Emordra! Don't give up!" Queen Ailith said as she tried to get the carpet to go faster.

It was the same day after Queen Ailith had returned to Argalon. She was making the dangerous trip to the Elgorn Forest in the hope that the forest would heal Emordra who had suddenly come down with a convulsion which the physicians could not handle. Looking at Emordra thrashing her limbs about spasmodically and frothing at the mouth as she maneuvered the carpet frantically, Queen Ailith knew it was only a matter of time before she gave up the ghost.

"Almost there," she said, suddenly plunging the carpet toward the forest.

In a short while they crashed onto the forest floor, sending a group of frightened birds flitting about. Rays of sunlight filtering through the leaves shone brightly onto Queen Ailith's face as she lay unconscious on the carpet with Emordra beside her, lifeless and with her tongue sticking out.

Coming to herself a short while later, Queen Ailith caught sight of Emordra. "Noooo!" she said, staggered up, knelt beside Emordra and began rousing her. "Wake up, Emordra! Wake up!"

Emordra did not respond.

"Help! Forest, help!" Queen Ailith shouted, frantically pressing on Emordra's chest.

Still there was no response.

For the next few minutes, Queen Ailith continued pressing on Emordra's chest, and when Emordra did not stir, she eventually gave up, buried her face in her hands hopelessly and began weeping. "Why couldn't you save her, forest? Why?" she said as she wailed. "She was all I had left."

As Queen Ailith continued weeping with her face buried in her hands, the most remarkable thing happened. She heard a cough, and when she removed her face from her hands, she caught sight of Emordra moving her limbs slowly with the lesions that were covering her body beginning to slowly disappear. Queen Ailith scoffed; she could not believe what she was seeing. Her scoff turned into laughter when Emordra eventually became whole before her eyes, her skin transforming into the healthy young woman Queen Ailith knew.

"Where am I? Where am I?" Emordra said after coming to herself.

"In the land of the living," Queen Ailith said.

Emordra sat up and noticed that the lesions and pus had disappeared from her body. "It can't be," she said and began examining her body.

"Yes, it can!" Queen Ailith replied, and just as she rose to her feet to thank the forest, they heard a loud trumpeting sound. "Oh, no," Queen Ailith said, the laughter fading immediately. She had heard that sound before, and she knew what it represented.

"What's that?" Emordra said.

"It's a Megaloth," Queen Ailith replied and they both caught sight of about ten Megaloths advancing toward them…slowly.

Emordra staggered to her feet. She and Queen Ailith stared at each other, and then joining hands together, unleashed a barrage of spears and darts. The spears and darts bounced off the Megaloths without harming them. Letting go of each other's hands, Emordra unleashed a lightning bolt; it was also useless. As if angered, the Megaloths started toward them fiercely.

"Run!" Queen Ailith said and she and Emordra turned and bolted.

Queen Ailith kicked behind her right leg and fell as they ran. Halting, Emordra turned and unleashed a series of lightning bolts to distract the Megaloths, which were now a few feet behind them, and then sprouting wings on her back, seized Queen Ailith and took off in flight. One of the Megaloths swung its proboscis, striking and breaking her wing. Emordra and Queen Ailith fell to the ground, and the Megaloths circled around them and touched their proboscis together, creating an energy field.

Queen Ailith and Emordra staggered back to their feet and began screaming as the Megaloths started sucking their souls. In that moment, they heard a loud pitching sound, and Queen Ailith and Emordra caught sight of some of the Megaloths flying back due to a strong force. Turning drunkenly, they caught sight of a gray-haired old man riding on a staff headed toward them; it was Egrane.

"Down!" Egrane said and unleashed a powerful force from the palms of his hands as Queen Ailith and Emordra bent down; the rest of the Megaloths went flying off and slammed into the nearby trees, which broke and slam into the ground.

"How did you know we were here?" Queen Ailith said after Egrane arrived and dismounted his staff.

"No time for questions. You must leave now," Egrane said breathlessly as he braced himself for the Megaloths that had risen up and were heading toward them.

"Not without you," Emordra said.

"Don't worry about me," Egrane replied and stretched forth his right hand which had his staff: a powerful force sprang out and kept the Megaloths at bay. "You must go. I cannot hold them off for long," Egrane said to Queen Ailith and Emordra who were still waiting. "Argalon needs you, not me," Egrane added.

"He's right, Emordra. We have to go," Queen Ailith said.

Emordra stared at Egrane, and after a brief hesitation, turned and joined Queen Ailith as they both began running out of the forest while looking over their shoulders. They were a good way off and almost at the edge of the forest when Egrane's power faded. Stopping and turning, they watched in tears as the Megaloths crowded around Egrane and began sucking out his soul using their proboscises. As the Megaloths continued sucking his soul, Egrane flung his staff to Queen Ailith and Emordra, saying they will need it.

Emordra grabbed the staff in midair and handed it to Queen Ailith.

"He was a great teacher," Queen Ailith said as she took the staff with tears streaming down her face.

"He was our father," Emordra replied with tears streaming down her face as well.

"Yes, he was like a father to us."

"No, I mean he was our *birth* father."

Queen Ailith turned and stared at Emordra, stunned. She could not believe what she was hearing.

Emordra stared back at her. "Mother told me, and she had wanted it to be kept a secret…"

TEARGHAD

"How come you never told me all these years?" Queen Ailith said with tears streaming down her face as Emordra walked over, wielding a burning torch.

It was a short while after they had made it home safely from the Elgorn Forest upon being rescued by Egrane. They were standing at King Debusis' grave in the backyard of the castle. Except for the thrilling cries of crickets echoing around, the night was silent and impenetrably dark.

"That King Debusis was not our father?" Emordra asked.

Queen Ailith nodded.

"Would you have accepted it had I told you?"

"At least you should have given me the choice."

A moment of silence engulfed them as they both stood staring at the grave. After a short while, Queen Ailith took closer steps to the grave, knelt down, and began weeping.

"I'm sorry you had to find out that way," Emordra said, walked up to Queen Ailith, knelt down beside her, and holding the torch in her left hand, began rubbing her right hand on her back.

"I no longer know who I am," Queen Ailith said, leaning her head onto Emordra's shoulder as she wept.

In that moment, a voice echoed saying, "You'll always be my daughters."

Startled, Queen Ailith and Emordra staggered to their feet and caught sight of a figure clothed in white standing on the grave.

"Is that you, father?" Queen Ailith asked, her voice trembling with fear.

"Yes," the ghost replied.

Weeping, Queen Ailith stretched her right hand to touch the ghost, but it forbade her. "No you can't touch me. It's against the rules."

Hesitating, Queen Ailith reluctantly lowered her hand.

Emordra, overwhelmed with sudden guilt and shame, recalled that fateful day when she choked King Debusis to death in his bed. "I'm sorry," she said faintly.

"The past is the past, Emordra. No need to be penitent," King Debusis' ghost replied, smiling at her. "I'm happy to see you two. Most importantly because for the first time you are joined together for a common cause," he added and then asked Queen Ailith and Emordra to follow him, saying he wanted to show them something.

Looking at each other questioningly, Queen Ailith and Emordra turned and followed their father's ghost as he got down from the grave and began leading them toward the castle wall.

As they walked, they caught sight of another ghost clad in white approaching from the east; it was their mother, Queen Zev.

"Mother?" Emordra said as she caught sight of the ghost.

Their mother had died of a terminal illness shortly before Egrane left Castle Argalona.

Queen Zev's ghost walked over, smiling. "How are you, Darlings?" she said and made to hug Emordra.

"You can't touch her," King Debusis' ghost interrupted.

"Oh, right," Queen Zev's ghost replied, restraining herself.

"We need to get going," King Debusis' ghost said. "We don't have much time."

"Where are you taking them?" Queen Zev's ghost asked.

King Debusis' ghost whispered in her ears.

"Oh, that's an exciting place," Queen Zev's ghost replied with a bright smile on her face. "Let's get going then," she added, and she and King Debusis turned and led the way, holding hands.

Queen Ailith and Emordra stared at each other questioningly once more and then followed behind their parent's ghosts.

Soon, they came up to the wall of the castle, and King Debusis' ghost said, "*Hakam Tatuum*!"

The ground suddenly began vibrating below them; the torch dropped from Emordra's hand and before she and Queen Ailith realized, the ground caved in below them, sending all four of them down a dark tunnel.

Queen Ailith and Emordra screamed as they fell down the tunnel, which appeared to be never ending. When they eventually reached to the end, they crashed into what appeared to be bags of hay in a dark place.

Panting and rising along with Queen Zev's ghost after crashing, King Debusis' ghost clapped and torches mounted on the walls lighted up, revealing a sprawling hall filled with arsenals. "Welcome to Tearghad, the vault of Argalon's defenses," he said, opening his arms.

"Wow," Queen Ailith and Emordra chorused in astonishment as they rose to take in the sights of rows upon rows of crossbows, shields, spears, swords, terracotta pots, bows and arrows and catapults.

King Debusis and Queen Zev's ghosts watched as Queen Ailith and Emordra walked up excitedly to the row of crossbows and began inspecting them.

"Who else knows about this place?" Queen Ailith asked, grabbing one of the crossbows.

"Only the king," King Debusis' ghost replied.

"And the queen," Queen Zev's ghost corrected.

King Debusis' ghost smiled at her. "And of course not forgetting my good friend, Spellus, the immortal guardian of Tearghad."

"Who's Spellus?" Emordra asked, reaching for a crossbow.

A hunched hobbit with gray, stringy hair and a pointed nose cleared his throat and walked over from between the rows with the spears. "I've been in much need of company for some time now," Spellus said softly as he walked over, and King Debusis' ghost introduced him to Queen Ailith and Emordra. "You've mentioned them to me in the past," Spellus said as Queen Ailith and Emordra walked up and shook his hand.

Letting go of each other's hands, Spellus asked whether Queen Ailith and Emordra wanted to see something magical.

"Sure!" Queen Ailith and Emordra replied enthusiastically.

With their parent's ghosts following behind, Spellus led Queen Ailith and Emordra over to the rows with the swords, pulled out a gold sword and handed it to Queen Ailith.

"That's my favorite," King Debusis' ghost said as Queen Ailith received the sword and began inspecting it; the sword looked ordinary except for a small knob on the hilt or handle.

"What's this knob?" Queen Ailith asked.

"Turn it," Spellus replied.

Queen Ailith turned the knob, and before she realized, the upper half of her body was covered in a shiny breastplate with a helmet on her head.

"Wow, a sword with an armor," Emordra said, her eyes gleaming.

"Yes, they are one," Spellus replied and asked Queen Ailith to rotate the knob again; Queen Ailith did, and the breastplate and helmet disappeared from around her body and head.

Spellus then reached his hand and pulled out another gold sword and handed it to Emordra.

"And that's *my* favorite," Queen Zev's ghost said as Emordra received the sword from Spellus.

"What does this do?" Emordra asked, inspecting the sword, and in that moment, the sword changed into a spear in her hand, startling her.

"That's not all," Spellus replied, and before Emordra realized, she was now holding a bow.

"Wow, a multipurpose weapon," Queen Ailith said.

"You haven't seen anything yet," Spellus said and asked Queen Ailith and Emordra to follow him.

Followed by their parent's ghosts once more, Spellus led Queen Ailith and Emordra to another row that had round iron balls that looked like apples with little keys on them. Spellus reached for one of the balls. "This is the cocoon," he said, pulled the key on its side and rolled it on the ground. "Stand back!" he commanded, and they all took cover behind the shelves while looking at the ball, which was spewing smoke as it rolled away, stopped and started bouncing repeatedly. Within a short while, it exploded and before Queen Ailith and Emordra realized, a towering three-headed beast with three pairs of wings on its back emerged out of the smoke, growling.

"Wow!" Queen Ailith and Emordra said, looking on excitedly.

They all stepped from behind the shelf as the creature flapped its wings and began flying about the hall, howling and breathing fire from its mouth. As the creature came toward them, Spellus took out a small cup from his pocket, opened it, and chanted: the creature grew small and entered the cup, leaving Queen Ailith and Emordra disappointed that he did not let the creature fly about for long.

As they watched the creature wriggle about in Spellus' cup, a whirlwind appeared out of nowhere.

Queen Ailith, Emordra and Spellus turned and caught sight of King Debusis and Queen Zev's ghosts being sucked into the wind.

"Father? Mother?" Queen Ailith and Emordra called.

"Our time is up," Queen Zev's ghost replied as she and King Debusis' ghosts were being sucked off. "We love you both!" she added.

"We love you too!" Queen Ailith and Emordra chorused.

"Go save Argalon!" King Debusis' ghost said before the whirlwind disappeared with them…

HE WHO IS WITHOUT SIN

The generals seated around the long table rose to their feet and bowed their heads briefly when Queen Ailith and Emordra, clad in partial armors, entered the Chamber of Swords and made their way to the heads of the table and sat down.

It was three days after Queen Ailith and Emordra's discovery of Tearghad through their parents' ghosts. Queen Ailith had called an urgent meeting with the generals in order to discuss the security threat facing Argalon and for them to prepare themselves for war.

"Thank you for gathering on such short notice," Queen Ailith began, clearing her throat as most of the generals looked at her, surprised and happy to see her back as queen. "I cannot begin to stress the gravity of the situation we find ourselves in…" she added, pausing in mid sentence, her eyes scanning the table. "Where is Grizen? And Rubius?" she asked.

All the generals seated at the table fixed their gaze on Emordra.

"I killed Grizen for killing Rubius," Emordra replied bluntly.

A moment of silence swept through the hall as Queen Ailith took in a deep breath and exhaled. "I suppose you're the ones who took their places," she said, pointing to two unfamiliar lads at the table.

"Yes," the two young men chorused and introduced themselves as Bearod and Damian, generals and rulers of the provinces of Marfa and Sud respectively.

"Were you not also the ones carrying out the war?" Queen Ailith asked.

"Yes," Bearod and Damian replied.

"But they've both made their peace and are here to help save Argalon," General Oryx interrupted from beside Pacifus.

Queen Ailith stared back and forth between Bearod and Damian and then resumed, stating that a fresh intelligence coming in has informed her that Mooran hordes had crossed into the kingdom of Argalon and were amassing forces in the Province of Ella.

"Should we seek the course of peace?" Pacifus interrupted.

"Had they wanted peace, they would have never sent Dutton to destabilize Argalon," Emordra said.

"Dutton? You mean Her Majesty's chief guard?" Quipps interrupted, shocked.

Queen Ailith nodded. "He's the Prince of Moora," she said.

"That bastard played us all for fools?" Beltus intoned, and in that moment they were interrupted by a loud voice echoing outside the hall.

"Who's that?" Queen Ailith said, and Romelot and Gazan entered the hall dragging Dutton behind them.

Dutton was bare-chested and had bruises and welts on his stomach and back, a result of the severe beatings he had endured while he was being held in the Mooran prison from which he had escaped.

"I demand to speak to Queen Ailith!" Dutton said as Romelot and Gazan dragged him in.

"Speaking of the devil," Emordra said, storming to her feet along with Generals Beltus, Akadie, Quipps, and Oryx who drew their swords.

"Traitor!" Quipps said and made to move swiftly toward Dutton with his sword stretched in front of him.

Emordra restrained him and motioned for the generals standing up to resume their seats.

Queen Ailith, who remained in her seat, was unsure what to do as she was astonished to see Dutton.

"You have some nerves coming back to Argalon after all what you did," Emordra said, walked up to Dutton, who was now standing and being restrained by Romelot and Gazan, and slapped him in his face.

"I have no quarrel with you, Emordra," Dutton said, without flinching. "My quarrel is with the queen."

"Your quarrel has everything to do with me and Argalon, bastard!" Emordra exploded, letting loose another slap across Dutton's face, and then turned to Queen Ailith. "What shall we do with him?"

Queen Ailith stared at Dutton, her breathing quickening; a part of her wanted to tear him up, but another part of her wanted to have mercy on him.

"You have to hear me out," Dutton said. "I was gamed by Vomesious. *He* murdered my parents."

"Shut up, Liar!" Emordra turned and backhanded Dutton. Afterwards she turned back to Queen Ailith. "What should we do with him?"

Queen Ailith took in a deep breath and let out a heavy sigh. "As you wish," she replied.

Dutton stared at Queen Ailith at the table as Emordra, grinning in satisfaction, turned and punched him in the face and stepped him in the stomach, sending him flying back along with Romelot and Gazan.

"That's how you deal with traitors!" Quipps said to a round of approval among Generals Akadie, Oryx and Beltus; the other generals seated at the table appeared indifferent to the situation. They had much love and respect for Dutton when he used to serve in the castle.

"It's enough!" Queen Ailith said, eventually storming to her feet as Romelot and Gazan rose up, grabbed hold of Dutton and lifted him up from the floor. "I want to talk to him alone. I want everyone out," She added.

Apart from Generals Pacifus, Casein, Dextrus and Vaga who rose up, the other generals remained seated, fuming.

"It's an order!" Queen Ailith said.

Reluctantly, the other generals rose up and filed out along with Generals Pacifus, Casein, Dextrus and Vaga, leaving Emordra, Romelot and Gazan.

"You too, Emordra," Queen Ailith said, walking up.

"Why?" Emordra said. "He lied and gamed us against each other. Besides, he is the one responsible for Argalon's problems. I want him dead."

Queen Ailith led Emordra aside and said, "I understand your anger, but I've got to talk to him alone."

"So you believe him?"

"I'm carrying his child."

Emordra gasped.

"I need this moment with him," Queen Ailith said.

After a short while, Emordra reluctantly agreed.

Queen Ailith motioned to Romelot and Gazan. They let go of Dutton and exited the hall along with Emordra who gave Dutton a stern look before reluctantly walking out. After Emordra, Romelot and Gazan exited the hall, there was silence between Queen Ailith and Dutton as they stared back at each other with a little distance between them.

"You don't have to forgive or show me mercy," Dutton broke the silence. "I only want you to hear me out."

Queen Ailith suddenly ran over to him, held him, kissed him passionately, and backhanded him after they let go of each other. "How dare you? How dare you use me and betray me?"

"You have every right to be angry with me," Dutton replied. "I don't deserve your mercy."

"I loved and trusted you, Dutton," Queen Ailith said, bursting into tears.

Dutton reached out to hold her, but she flinched. "Why did you come back?" she asked.

"Redemption. All I want is to be given the chance to clear my conscience and help right the wrongs I committed against the woman that I love and her people."

Queen Ailith scoffed. "You fooled me once; why should I trust you now?"

"Because this time around, I'm standing before you without a mask on."

Queen Ailith gasped and rubbed her hands through her hair. "Out there, there are angry generals who would love to see you sent to the gallows. What do I say to them?"

"Do what your heart says."

Queen Ailith scoffed. "My heart?" she said, and for a moment, there was silence between them as she stared into Dutton's eyes. She moved in after a short while and kissed him. Afterwards, she said, "I have to give the people of Argalon justice, and justice is greater than my feelings toward you. I'll have to let the generals decide your fate."

"Fair enough," Dutton said, closing his eyes and clenching his teeth; deep down in his heart he had hoped Queen Ailith would pardon him.

"I'm sorry," Queen Ailith said and called out to the generals to come back in.

"Whatever happens, I want you to know that you are a great queen, Ailith, and that I was honored to have served you," Dutton said as the generals filed back in along with Emordra and resumed their seats.

Queen Ailith stared at Dutton, turned, walked over and sat back at the head of the table.

"So what's the course of action going to be?" Quipps said as soon as Queen Ailith resumed her seat.

"It's yours to decide," Queen Ailith replied.

"I say death at the gallows!" Quipps said.

Queen Ailith scanned the faces of the generals along with Emordra. "Is that what you all want?"

"No," General Pacifus replied, and then said to the other generals, "Comrades, we have all done things in the past that we were never proud of. If Dutton honestly came seeking forgiveness, it's only fitting that he be forgiven…"

"Nonsense! He's a traitor!" Quipps interrupted.

"If you're without sin, cast the first stone, Quipps," Pacifus replied.

"Why do you always have to say something cowardly?" Quipps shot back.

"Just because I'm a lover of peace does not necessarily make me a coward," Pacifus replied.

"You are a coward, Pacifus," Oryx interrupted.

"Enough!" Queen Ailith, surprised that Emordra was not saying anything, interrupted. "Those in favor of death raise your hands."

Quipps' hand shot up along with Bados, Oryx, Beltus and Damian; they were five in number, leaving seven generals' hands down.

Queen Ailith scanned the faces of the rest of the generals who had their hands down including Emordra. "Anybody else?" she asked.

None of the generals who had their hands down raised theirs, not even Emordra, surprising Quipps and his allies.

Dutton uttered a sigh of relief.

"I think it's clear the majority wishes him to live," Queen Ailith said and called out to Romelot and Gazan who entered the hall. "Usher Dutton out and give him food to eat and a robe to wear."

As Romelot and Gazan led Dutton out, Queen Ailith leaned in to Pacifus who was sitting beside her and said, "Thank you for saving his life for me."

Pacifus grinned, and afterwards, they turned their attention to war...

PREBATTLE (LETTER EXCHANGES)

From the Argalonian encampment close to the battlefield...

Queen Ailith's letter to Vomesious: *"Vomesious, King of Moora, I advise you to abandon this enterprise, for it will do you no good in the end. Rule your people and leave me to rule mine. I know, however, that you will refuse my advice as the last thing you want is to live in peace, or why else would you device such elaborate conspiracy. If that be the case, be forewarned; my people and I are ready to defend our land and kingdom at all cost and swear to give you more blood than you can drink for all your evil and treachery!"*

King Vomesious' reply: *"Nothing is going to set me off my course. Not even your timid rants. I assure you, Argalon shall cease being a kingdom and become history tomorrow. Moreover, Moora shall become an empire in Lothian, and I shall become its immortal ruler and god, feared and worshipped by many!..."*

Queen Ailith's reply: "*I see that you are a mad man whose delusions have no cure. There's only one place for people like you—the Underworld. And that's exactly where my forces and I would send you and your forces by sundown tomorrow!*"

King Vomesious' reply: "*Ha, don't you see how pathetic you sound, weak and petty queen? I shall give you a glorious and painful death before the eyes of your people after I vanquish your forces tomorrow; I shall rape you and have that traitorous lover of yours Dutton watch in agony and pain while hanging from the gallows, and then afterwards, I shall disembowel you and feed your innards to my dogs!*"

Queen Ailith's reply: "*Now I know that you are not only mad but also a psychopath!*"

King Vomesious' reply: "*Now I know that you are not only weak, but a coward! See you on the battlefield tomorrow and come ready to die along with your kingdom…*"

BATTLE FOR ELLA

"Death to the Kingdom of Argalon! Death to the Kingdom of Argalon!..." dressed in yellow battle regalia and wielding shields, swords, battle axes and spears, thousands upon thousands of Mooran soldiers chanted frenziedly in the valley with the spirit of war upon them.

It was noon, but the sky above was ominously dark. Queen Ailith, clad in full battle regalia with a helmet under her right arm, sat on a white horse perched atop a small hill, staring down the valley at the Mooran position with a grave look on her face. The sight of the innumerable Mooran army stretching in the valley like grains of sand on a seashore struck terror in her heart. Her forces, lined up about twenty feet behind her on the hill, were numbered two to one!

As Queen Ailith continued staring down at the Mooran position with a kettle of vultures circling about repeatedly in the gloomy rain-laden sky, two black horses cantered from behind and joined her on the hill, each horse taking to her flank. The horses were mounted by Emordra and Dutton, both of whom were fully armored.

For a moment, there was silence between them as they all stared down at the Mooran position with grave looks on their faces.

"Are the men ready?" Queen Ailith eventually broke the silence a short while later, looking straight ahead of her.

"Yes," Emordra replied.

"And the archers?" Queen Ailith asked.

"They are all ready," Emordra replied. "I only await your signal to unleash hell on these pests."

Queen Ailith continued staring down the Mooran position, and then a short while later, turned her horse around and trotted toward the thousands of Argalonian soldiers who were dressed in red and white battle regalia and wielding spears, shields, clubs and bows and arrows. The generals, who were mounted on horses in front of the soldiers, were wielding spears and staffs with Argalonian flags tied to them. Emordra and Dutton followed behind Queen Ailith and took to her flanks as she approached the army, stopped and began scanning through the ranks who looked upon her, awaiting a word.

"Fellow Argalonians," Queen Ailith suddenly called out as her horse reared under her, "I stand before you on this momentous day in our history not as your queen, but as your fellow warrior, a comrade in arms. Our hearts beat with the same fire: the survival of Argalon. On the battlefield, we shall bleed the same blood. When you strike, I will strike with you. When you fall, I will fall with you. And in life or death, we shall be borne by the same spirit, always!" she added, drawing her sword from her side and thrusting it into the air. "Long live Argalon!"

"Long live Argalon!" Emordra, Dutton, the generals and soldiers shouted, thrusting their varied weapons into the air as the spirit of war ceased them.

Placing her helmet on her head, Queen Ailith turned to Emordra to her left. "You know what to do."

"Archers! Catapult shooters!" Emordra cried out and all of a sudden a group of soldiers wielding bows and arrows, terracotta pots and dragging catapults scurried from behind the ranks and ran past them to the top of the hill.

As the archers and catapult shooters scurried to the top of the hill, Queen Ailith, Emordra, Dutton, the generals and the soldiers caught sight of a cloud of dust rising to their east.

"What the bloody hell is that?" Queen Ailith said as she, Emordra and Dutton cantered their horses to the eastern edge of the army.

Soon a pack of wolves led by a female rider emerged from the dust.

"Mena," Queen Ailith said, smiling after catching sight of the rider.

"Who's Mena?" Emordra asked.

"A friend of mine," Queen Ailith replied.

Within a short time, Mena and her pack of wolves arrived. "I thought I was never going to make it in time," she said breathlessly and then greeted Queen Ailith and Dutton.

Queen Ailith introduced her to Emordra.

"What are you doing here?" Queen Ailith asked Mena after she and Emordra exchanged pleasantries.

"We heard you were on the warpath, so Lord Petreus sent me to aid your cause."

"Lord Petreus? Where is he?"

"Sick, but he should be fine."

They were interrupted by a loud trumpet blast from the Mooran camp.

"Battle time!" Dutton said, as he and Emordra turned their horses and rode toward the archers and catapult shooters perched atop the hill, leaving Queen Ailith and Mena.

Upon arriving on the hill, Emordra and Dutton caught sight of Moorans shouting at the top of their lungs running toward them with full speed.

The archers and the catapult shooters readied themselves by flaming their arrow tips and the terracotta pots while awaiting Emordra's signal.

"Unleash!" Emordra commanded within a short while as the Moorans approached to within about one hundred eighty yards.

The archers and catapult shooters unleashed a storm of flaming arrows and terracotta pots upon the Moorans.

The effect was immediate: Moorans screamed and fell as they were picked up repeatedly by the arrows and as the terracotta pots exploded among them.

Undaunted, the Moorans kept coming, however.

Upon Emordra's command, the archers and catapult shooters sent another barrage of flaming arrows and terracotta pots flying into the midst of the Moorans, who kept running toward them on full speed and screaming at the top of their lungs despite being picked up repeatedly by the arrows and terracotta pots.

Soon Queen Ailith, Mena, the generals and the soldiers moved to the top of the hill along with the pack of wolves.

"To Argalon!" Queen Ailith said, thrusting her sword into the air.

"To Argalon!" everybody shouted around her, thrusting their weapons into the air.

"Charge!" Queen Ailith commanded, pointing her sword in front her as they descended the hill to meet the onrushing Moorans and began slashing their way brutally through them, sending blood splattering about and body parts flinging around.

Queen Ailith chopped off the head of a Mooran who approached her horse and stabbed the neck of another as Emordra, Dutton and Mena, who were flanking her to her right and left, slashed through the Moorans with the pack of wolves feasting happily on their flesh.

The Moorans fought back with equal brutality, spearing and chopping off the heads of Argalonian soldiers.

It was carnage, and for the next few minutes the fight raged on fiercely without any side gaining a significant advantage.

Queen Ailith had just stepped a Mooran to the ground and thrust her sword into his chest when she caught sight of a fleet of grotesque, large-winged lizards, swooping toward them. "The cocoons! Unleash the cocoons!" she shouted.

The blood-covered generals around her reached into their armors, brought out the cocoons, pulled the keys from them and rolled the balls on the ground.

"Stand back! Stand back!" Emordra ordered and the Argalonian soldiers gave way as the balls rolled off spewing smoke.

The Mooran soldiers were confused as they looked upon the little balls bouncing around them and spewing smoke.

Soon the balls started exploding around them and out came the three-headed beasts with the three pairs of wings.

"Feast!" Emordra ordered and the three-headed beasts started devouring the Moorans soldiers as some of them took to the skies after the grotesque, large-winged lizards and started devouring them too.

Inundated and taken by surprise, the Moorans soldiers started dropping their swords and fleeing. The wolves and the Argalonian forces chased after them, hacking away at their heads as Dutton went in search of King Vomesious on his horse.

"King Vomesious, where the bullocks are you?" he called as he rode around among the fleeing Moorans, seething with the thought of revenge.

King Vomesious was nowhere to be found…

At last, the battle ended, and when the dust began to settle, it was Argalon who remained standing. They had won, but had suffered heavy casualties, leaving only a few thousand men. Of the generals, only Quipps had fallen.

Queen Ailith, Emordra, Dutton, Mena, the rest of the generals and the Argalonian soldiers, bathed in blood and battle spent, galloped through the corpse-laden field, surveying the aftermath of the battle in silence and with grave looks on their faces.

There was nothing pretty about the sights. All around them there was death.

"Did you find him?" Queen Ailith said to Dutton who was riding to her left.

"King Vomesious?" Dutton replied.

Queen Ailith nodded.

"No. I suppose he escaped," Dutton replied and in that moment, they were interrupted by a loud voice echoing not too far from them.

A Mooran survivor whose legs had been hacked off began hurling curses on them. "Bloody fools! You've been deceived! You shall all die along with your kingdom!" he cried out.

Dutton moved swiftly and thrust his sword into his heart. As he rode back, General Bados raised the Argalon ode. The other generals and soldiers joined him, lifting their mood.

"O hail, mighty Argalon! Long live thy holy name!" they sang, heartily. "May generations to come forever know you! May the blood spilled by our forefathers in birthing you never go in vain! And may all, standing together in unity, forever defend you even at the cost of our lives! Hail, mighty Argalon! Long live thy name!"

As they sang repeatedly, the rain descended in full force, drenching them. They went around in the rain, picking up their wounded from around the battlefield along with the corpse of General Quipps, and afterwards, rode back toward Castle Argalona in victory, leaving the vultures, the wolves and the three-headed beasts to feast merrily on the dead...

BATTLE FOR ARAVON I

The city of Aravon, which was the capital city of the Kingdom of Argalon, was gripped with fear and mass hysteria as fleets of warships ambulating on the Nubian Ocean inched closer to their coast.

Queen Ailith and Dutton stood on the balcony of Castle Argalona looking toward sea with grave looks on their faces. Tired and spent, it was shortly after they had returned from the Battle of Ella. Not even the bravest warrior among them could summon up the courage at the crushing and ominous sight of what was coming toward them.

"It appears your allies, Varanasi and Sorovan, have joined forces with Moora," Dutton said, pointing to the green and white flags clearly visible among the fleet of warships from the balcony of Castle Argalona.

The sky above was bathed in a pink and orange glow as the sun made its gradual retreat to the night in the evening sky. But to the west grave storm clouds were moving in.

Queen Ailith and Dutton were interrupted when Emordra walked out from inside the castle. "The generals are gathered in the hall, as you requested," she said and stood beside Queen Ailith. "They are all worried," she added.

Without saying a word, Queen Ailith turned and began heading back into the castle; Emordra and Dutton followed her.

As she entered the hall with Dutton and Emordra behind her, the generals seated at the table rose to their feet and bowed to her.

"No need for formalities. You may all rise and sit," Queen Ailith said.

The Generals rose to their feet and resumed their seats as Queen Ailith, Emordra and Dutton walked to the table and took their seats; Romelot, Gazan and a handful of guards were standing guard around the hall.

"Gentlemen, I know we are all tired and spent from the Battle at Ella. But all our labors and the deaths of our comrades such as General Quipps would amount to nothing if we do not rise over our fears and finish the work we started," Queen Ailith began immediately after taking her seat, and then paused, scanning the faces of the generals who looked back at her with grave expressions. "This is the land our forefathers bequeathed to us through their blood and sacrifices and we are not going to be the ones to let it fall to our enemies—certainly not on our time!" she said, tapping her index finger on the table before her. "Emordra," she called. "Gather the archers on the towers, parapets, drawbridge, gatehouse, and the temple."

"As you wish," Emordra replied.

"Damian, Bados, Orxy and Beltus," she called, "I want you all to lead about two thousand of your men to give our enemies a bloody welcome to our shores. You shall be our first line of defense."

"Yes, Your Majesty," the generals mentioned chorused.

"The rest of you shall stay here with me."

"Yes, Your Majesty," the remaining generals chorused.

Queen Ailith scanned the general's faces, took in a deep breath and exhaled. "Comrades, I'm under no illusions and know that it's a daunting task before us. As a result, many of us would not make it through this storm. Should we meet in the afterlife, however, may the blessings of our ancestors accompany us all. But before then, may our individual courage and actions today forever echo!" She then rose from her seat, drew her sword, and stretched it before her. "Long live Argalon!"

The generals, whose spirits had been awakened, stormed to their feet, drew their swords, and stretched it before them with their tips touching Queen Ailith's. "Long live Argalon!" they shouted and then dispersed.

As the generals exited, Romelot walked up to Queen Ailith. "I come to ask for your forgiveness, Highness, for my treachery against you."

Queen Ailith grinned. "Forgiveness does not change the past, Romelot; it changes the future," she said. "I hope you will make better choices in the future."

"Certainly!" Romelot said, bowed and left.

Dutton walked up to Queen Ailith as Romelot left. "What would you have me do, Your Majesty?" he said.

"I always feel safe with you by my side," Queen Ailith replied. "Lead me to the temple," she added, and Dutton led her out of the hall.

The temple was crowded with women, children, and old men. The citizenry who had gathered there in huge numbers seeking refuge from the advancing enemy forces cried out to Queen Ailith as she walked in with Dutton behind her.

"Save us, Your Majesty! Save us from the wrath of our enemies!" they cried to her repeatedly as she walked between them, went and stood in front of them with Dutton by her side and motioned for silence.

The people immediately quieted down, looking upon Queen Ailith with hope in their eyes. She had a way with them that made them love and revere her. During the second year of her reign, she had reversed a severe famine that had gripped the Kingdom of Argalon, leading the people to build her the temple, erect a statue in her honor and worship her as the Goddess Vera personified. (Vera was the Argalonian goddess of love and war whom Queen Ailith served as Priestess in her teen years). If at all anybody could save them once more, they believed it was Queen Ailith.

"I understand your fears!" Queen Ailith said as the people looked upon her. "But I must say, we Argalonians are not a people of fear! I assure you we will survive this and vanquish our enemies!"

"Yaaaaaa!" some of the people chanted.

"Long live Argalon!" Queen Ailith shouted, pushing the air with her clenched fist.

"Long live Argalon! Long live Argalon!" the peopled chanted repeatedly and burst forth into the Argalonian ode.

"O hail, mighty Argalon! Long live thy holy name!" they sang heartily along with Queen Ailith. "May generations to come forever know you! May the blood spilled by our forefathers in birthing you never go in vain! And may all, standing together in unity, forever defend you even at the cost of our lives! Hail, mighty Argalon! Long live thy name!"

As the people continued singing vociferously, Queen Ailith and Dutton turned and entered into a small room to the right.

Leaving Dutton at the entrance to the room, Queen Ailith walked forward and fell before Vera's altar. "Vera," she said, "I know we might have parted ways and forsaken each other sometime in the distant past, but I need you now. Argalon needs you. If you are there give me a sign that you are with us."

There was no reply.

"Please Vera, please," she said; still there was no reply.

"Where are the gods when you need them?" she rose to her feet in frustration a short while later and turned to Dutton at the door. "We pray and offer them sacrifices yet they often neglect us in our darkest hours when we most need them."

Dutton stared at her, unsure what to say or do; things had been happening so fast since his return to Argalon to the point that they had barely spoken to each other about anything else except the war. He wondered how the baby she was carrying was coming on.

"Why Vera? Why do you abandon me at the hour of my need?" Queen Ailith said, turned around, picked up a calabash from the altar and slammed it into the wall. She then reached for Vera's idol, which was made from clay, from the altar, broke it into pieces and threw it down. Afterwards, she fell to her knees, buried her face in her hands and burst forth into tears.

Dutton walked up to her and held her in his arms as she wept.

They were interrupted in that moment as Emordra walked into the room. "I bring you grave news," she said upon entering into the chamber.

Wiping her face with the heel of her hand, Queen Ailith rose to her feet. "Speak," she said, turning to Emordra.

"The coast has been overrun. Beltus, Oryx, Bados and Damian are all dead."

"So quickly?" Queen Ailith said, sniffing.

"I'm afraid so," Emordra replied, adding that the enemies were headed toward the castle.

Queen Ailith lowered her head despondently and let out a heavy sigh.

"We need to head back into the walls of the castle," Emordra said.

"I shall remain here with the people and die with them."

"No. No, sister. I can't let you do that. Right, Dutton?" Emordra said.

Dutton nodded.

Queen Ailith stared into Emordra's eyes and then Dutton's. "All right," she replied reluctantly, and just as Emordra and Dutton were about to lead her away, the most surprising thing happened: a hand appeared onto the wall in front of them and began writing.

"Use Egrane's staff," Emordra read out the writing as the hand disappeared. "For what?" she said.

Queen Ailith grinned for she knew that Vera had answered her at last...

BATTLE FOR ARAVON II

"Charge!" the command rang out and hundreds of undaunted enemy soldiers screaming at the top of their lungs ran and pummeled the main gate with battering rams in their attempt to enter the castle ground.

Queen Ailith, standing at the bay window in a chamber of the castle with Egrane's staff in her hand, watched with a grave look on her face with Dutton beside her. As they stood at the window, they could hear Emordra shouting orders as hails of flaming arrows and burning terracotta pots rained down on the enemies ceaselessly from the towers and parapets, picking them up in numbers.

Yet the enemies refused to budge and continued pummeling the gate.

"I know I have hardly said a word to you since the generals pardoned you, but I want you to know that I feel safe with you by my side," Queen Ailith said after a series of thunder storms clapped in the rain-laden night sky.

"I owe you and Argalon my life," Dutton replied. "It's because of my actions that Argalon has come to this," he added.

"You're not to blame, Dutton," Queen Ailith replied. "We are all in some way responsible for everything happening today. We made choices which we believed apt in our eyes. You only did what you did because you believed in justice."

Dutton stared into Queen Ailith's eyes; she stared into his as well as the burning torches mounted on the walls of the chamber flickered in their eyes.

"The child you are carrying…how is it?" Dutton asked.

"Growing," Queen Ailith replied, chuckled and reached for Dutton's right hand and placed it on her stomach. "Can you feel it?"

Dutton nodded, smiling. "I give you my word. No matter what happens here tonight the two of you shall not fall—not while I have breath in me."

Queen Ailith smiled, and as she reached in to kiss Dutton, an arrow suddenly whizzed through the bay window. Dutton instinctively pulled Queen Ailith to the right after catching sight of the incoming arrow through the corner of his eye; the arrow caught his left arm as two of them went tumbling to the ground with the staff falling from Queen Ailith's hand.

In that moment, Emordra ran into the chamber. "I need to get you to the basement now," she said, breathless. "They've breeched the defenses."

As Dutton rolled from over Queen Ailith, Emordra noticed the arrow sticking in his arm. "You got caught," she said.

"I'll be fine," Dutton replied, and with his teeth clenched together, pulled the arrow from his arm as Queen Ailith staggered to her feet.

A series of arrows whizzed into the chamber.

"We need to go now," Emordra said, and they began running out of the chamber.

"Wait. The staff," Queen Ailith said, halting as they got to the door.

"Hurry," Emordra said, and Queen Ailith ran back to pick up the staff.

As Queen Ailith reached for the staff from the ground, they heard a loud hysterical laugh and King Vomesious appeared into the chamber, clad in a black robe

"At last, we meet...again, Lyra," King Vomesious said mockingly, and then suddenly sent Queen Ailith flying into the wall with a lightning bolt; Queen Ailith crashed into the wall with the staff in her hand and fell to the ground.

Dutton immediately unsheathed his sword and uttering a shrill cry came running toward King Vomesious. King Vomesious stretched forth his hand, which lengthened like a rope, and grabbed Dutton by his neck. "I will kill you like I killed your father," he said and flung Dutton across the chamber; Dutton landed beside Queen Ailith, grunting in pain. "Where is the Philosopher's Stone?" King Vomesious asked.

Furious, Emordra swung her hair, the boa constrictors on her head lengthened and wrapped around King Vomesious' neck, clenching and choking him. "Dutton, get my sister out of here and leave this wretch to me!" she said as King Vomesious struggled to free himself from the boa constrictors.

Dutton staggered to his feet along with Queen Ailith, and limping, they both started running out of the chamber with the staff.

Queen Ailith stopped at the door and looked back at Emordra. "And you?" she said.

"Go!" Emordra replied.

Hesitating, Queen Ailith joined Dutton as they both ran out of the chamber.

"You've met your match," Emordra said, walking over to King Vomesious who fell to the ground as the snakes uncoiled from around him and returned to her head elastically.

"Not quite," King Vomesious said, sending Emordra flying into the wall with a powerful force shooting from his palm.

Emordra crashed into the wall, fell to the ground, staggered back to her feet almost instantly and unleashed a series of spears which King Vomesious did well to evade by rolling away on the ground. Before King Vomesious could stagger back up, Emordra, screaming at the top of her lungs like a mad person, ran, leapt up into the air and landed on his head with her right knee. Screaming, King Vomesious pushed Emordra away, staggered up and swung his right hand at her; Emordra dodged, kneed him in his stomach and sent him flying into the wall with a lightning bolt.

Meanwhile, after Dutton and Queen Ailith exited the chamber, on their way to the basement, they came across Romelot, Gazan, Pacifus and a handful of Argalonian soldiers battling a large number of enemy soldiers in a sprawling hall.

Dutton and Queen Ailith immediately joined the fight, swinging and slashing at the enemies who kept screaming and coming toward them in droves.

Queen Ailith stepped an enemy soldier in the chest and swung her staff at his head. Dutton chopped off the head of another soldier, and afterwards, he, Romelot, Pacifus, Gazan and three other Argalonian soldiers formed a circle around Queen Ailith and fought to protect her.

Back in the chamber, the fight raged between Emordra and King Vomesious. Emordra, who was now wielding a sword, swung fiercely at king Vomesious who, also wielding a sword, blocked her every strike as fire sparked fiercely from their blades.

"Today, you die," Emordra said breathlessly, knocked King Vomesious' sword from his hand, punched him in the nose and kneed him in his stomach. Uttering a shrill cry, King Vomesious bent over to hold his stomach; Emordra kicked him in the face, sending him flying to the ground. Not wanting to give him any respite, Emordra moved swiftly toward King Vomesious to decapitate him; King Vomesious stretched forth his hand, sending Emordra flying into the opposite wall with a lightning bolt. Emordra immediately staggered back to her feet after crashing into the wall and unleashed a series of poison darts, one of which caught King Vomesious on his left thigh as the rest whizzed by him narrowly.

King Vomesious uttered a piercing and agonizing cry as Emordra walked up to him. "That dart," she said, "is a poison dart. It kills slowly by paralyzing its victim and causing blood to ooze out of his mouth, nose, ears and eyes while his innards burn as if they were on fire. Afterwards, he shall explode. You, Vomesious, will die a slow and painful death."

With that said, Emordra turned to walk away. Sensing an opportunity to strike back, King Vomesious quickly reached for his dagger from his side and flung it saying, "You shall die with me, you whore!"

Emordra, who did not see the dagger coming, could not react in time; the dagger pierced her in the back. She fell to her knees. "Desire, how many lives have been consumed by your burning flame?" she said, uttered a brief laugh and fell face down to the ground as blood poured from her.

Pulling the dart from his thigh, King Vomesious staggered agonizingly to his feet and labored out of the chamber to go in search of Queen Ailith and the Philosopher's Stone which he knew was the only thing that could save him from the poison of the dart.

As he exited the chamber, King Vomesious caught sight of Queen Ailith and Dutton, who were covered in blood, running toward him as a number of his soldiers, who had killed Pacifus, Romelot and Gazan, pursued them. Queen Ailith and Dutton halted upon seeing King Vomesious ahead of them; they both knew that moment that Emordra was dead.

"Where is the Philosopher's Stone?" King Vomesious said after commanding his soldiers to halt their advances toward Queen Ailith and Dutton.

"You bastard! You killed my sister. Prepare to die," Queen Ailith said and made to move toward King Vomesious, but Dutton restrained her.

"You want the Philosopher's Stone?" Dutton said. "It's in the Chamber of Swords."

King Vomesious stared at Dutton with a mocking look on his face. "The prince who gave up his position for a cheap whore, defying his own king and uncle in the process. What a fantastic story. Now we'll all like to know how that story ends—"

"Do you want the stone or not?" Dutton interrupted.

"Of course," King Vomesious said.

"Follow me," Dutton said as Queen Ailith stared at him questioningly, wondering what he was doing.

King Vomesious nodded to one of his soldiers who moved swiftly, grabbed hold of Queen Ailith and put a dagger to her throat. "I'll kill her if you try to game me," King Vomesious said and ordered his guards to give way.

As Dutton turned to lead the way to the Chamber of Swords, they heard a loud scream and what appeared to be a long rope curled around

King Vomesious' neck and began chocking him. Turning, Dutton caught sight of Emordra; it was the snakes from her head that were choking King Vomesious.

"I'm not dead yet!" Emordra said and began pulling King Vomesious toward her as his eyes bulged.

Dutton immediately grabbed a sword from a nearby soldier and thrust it into the neck of the soldier holding Queen Ailith hostage; afterwards, he and Queen Ailith began fighting the rest of the soldiers around them.

As they fought the soldiers, the hand that Queen Ailith had seen in the temple earlier appeared and began writing on the wall. *Strike the ground with the staff*, the hand wrote. A group of soldiers scrambled to prevent Queen Ailith from striking the ground with the staff, but it was late. Queen Ailith struck the ground with the staff. For a moment nothing happened as everyone gathered around froze as if waiting to see what will happen. Within a short while, a bright and immense force swept through the hall and everything went into darkness...

BATTLE FOR ARAVON III

When Queen Ailith opened her eyes, she found herself lying in the courtyard of the castle with sun rays flashing into her eyes. Dutton was beside her, lying unconscious with his sword and Egrane's staff beside him. Not too far away, King Vomesious was lying face down on the ground along with Emordra and the soldiers. As Queen Ailith staggered to her feet, she noticed the castle floating on the sea without any land or coast in sight.

"It can't be," she said in astonishment as she looked around at the vast sea around her. She had just reached over to rouse Dutton when a force hit her, sending her to the ground. As she fell, she caught sight of King Vomesious standing a few feet from her.

"This is where it all ends for you and Argalon," King Vomesious said, and stretched his right hand to unleash a lightning bolt; his hand stuck and no lightning bolt came out. Surprised, he tried to move his hand, but was unable to. Instead, his body began vibrating spasmodically and blood started oozing out of his eyes, nose, and ears; the poison from Emordra's dart was beginning to work on him. Dutton, who had regained consciousness by now, grabbed his sword from the ground, rose up, and uttering a shrill cry, ran over to King Vomesious and thrust his sword into his chest, pulled the sword out and thrust it once more while saying, "This is for killing my parents!"

He watched as King Vomesious gave a faint grin and burst open, sending his innards and body parts flying about. Queen Ailith, who had been watching, rose to her feet and ran over to Emordra when she caught sight of her stirring slowly.

"Emordra!" she called as she ran over, knelt beside her and held her hand.

Emordra raised her blood-covered hand slowly and touched Queen Ailith's cheek. "M-my time has come," she whimpered.

"Please don't die," Queen Ailith said and began weeping as Dutton joined her and Emordra.

"Take care of my sister for me," Emordra said to Dutton.

Dutton nodded.

"Long live Argalon," Emordra said with a faint grin and let out the ghost.

"Noooooooooo!" Queen Ailith screamed, bursting out into tears as Dutton moved swiftly and began thrusting his sword into the necks of a couple of soldiers he caught stirring on the floor. Afterwards, he came back and tried to console Queen Ailith. Queen would not be consoled. As she wept and wept, she was reminded of the day Emordra saved her life. They were eight years old then. They had gone out for a ride on Emordra's broom shortly after Egrane had given her the broom as a gift. Egrane had warned them to not go riding on the broom until they had mastered its use. But Emordra convinced Ailith, and they both sneaked out through her room window and went flying over Argalon. It was a sunny day, and the air was crisp. They were enjoying their ride, flying about five hundred feet above sea level, when Ailith suddenly slipped from the broom and began hurtling toward the ground screaming. Emordra swooped for her, stretched forth her hand and caught her just as she was about to fall onto a peg on a farm.

"I will never let you fall," Emordra said as she helped frightened Ailith onto the broom with a smile on her face and shot back toward the castle. "I will never let you fall."

The thought brought a faint smile on Queen Ailith's face; that was typical Emordra, she thought.

She was drawn out of her thoughts when Dutton asked her how they were going to get back.

Queen Ailith turned and looked at the staff which was lying not too far from them. Rising reluctantly, she walked up to the staff, grabbed it, and slammed it on the ground, but nothing happened. She tried again but nothing happened once more. Dropping the staff, she walked back to Dutton. "I don't know," she said.

Dutton stared at her, and an inevitable thought crossed his mind; he knew they were lost, and perhaps with no chance of ever going back. He walked up to Queen Ailith and hugged her. "It's going to be alright. We're going to be alright," he said as they both clung to each other with tears streaming down their faces.

They were interrupted by a loud roar as they clung to each other. Letting go of each other, they caught sight of a four-headed creature with numerous tentacles rising from the sea and heading toward them.

"What the bloody hell is that?" Queen Ailith said as she and Dutton braced for the incoming creature...

POLITICAL MAP OF LOTHIAN

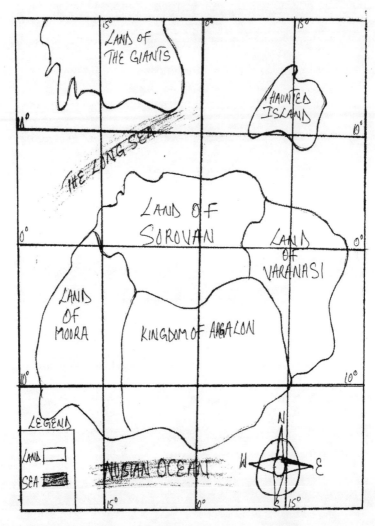

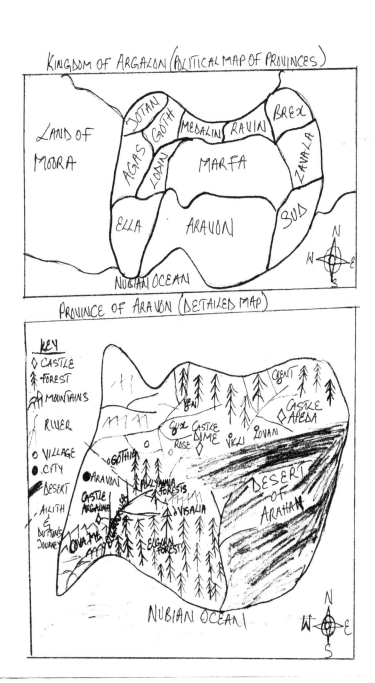

Kingdom of Argalon (Political Map of Provinces)

Province of Aravon (Detailed Map)

TIMELINE and GENEOLOGY

- Bisc 2301   Degas, the founder of Argalon, is born on a ship that eventually sinks on the Nubian Ocean on a dark and stormy night. A little kindness from the people of Argal in rescuing him would later serve them well as he would grow up to become their savior.

- Bisc 2316 -- Argal is conquered by King Jujides of the North and his armies; the people of Argal are led into captivity.

- Bisc 2331 -- Degas leads a successful slave rebellion against King Jujides of the North and his armies; the emancipated slaves move back southward on the Trail of Blood and resettle in their previous land of Argal, renaming it Argalon. And with that, Argalon is born!

- Bisc 2331 -- Two days after its birth, Argalon survives a fierce attack from the Gruls.

- Bisc 2332 -- Degas begins the expansion of Argalon by conquering the Land of Cova and annexing it's territory.

- Bisc 2335 -- Degas builds the Vogumgata for sports.

- Bisc 2336 -- Degas conquers the Land of the Gruls, and annexes it, renaming it the Province of Ella after his wife.

- Bisc 2337 -- Degas' son and eventual successor, Bavus, is born.

- Bisc 2338 - 2341 -- Degas conquers and annexes the Lands of Varus, Wunderborough and Jos, renaming them the provinces of Sud, Lodin and Agas respectively.

- Bisc 2344 -- Kings Cervas, Gradus and Lukis form a pact with Argalon, annexing their territories of Marfa, Zavala and Brex respectively.

- Bisc 2354 -- The Land of Moora attacks Argalon, but is beating back by the Argalonians; Degas dies during this time. His son Bavus, ascends the throne.

- Bisc 2359 -- Bavus conquers and annexes the territories of Grinx and Duvs, renaming them Goth and Jotan.

- Bisc 2360 -- Rongas, Bavus' son and successor, is born.

- Bisc 2386 -- Rongas murders his father Bavus and assumes the throne.

- Bisc 2387 - 2394 -- Liffet and Rus, Rongas' sons, are born.

- Bisc 2426 -- Liffet and Rus defeat their father Rongas at the Battle of Gunrus; Liffet murders his brother Rus after that and assumes his throne.

- Bisc 2427 -- Liffet gives birth to Goran.
- Bisc 2459 -- Liffet dies and Goran assumes the throne.
- Bisc 2460 -- Goran conquers and annexes the Lands of Medalin and Ravin.
- Bisc 2468 --Goran's daughter Icatra is born.
- Bisc 2490 --Icatra assumes the throne after Goran's death
- Bisc 2491 -- Icatra gives birth to Loas
- Bisc 2518 -- Loas son, Kangas, is born; Icatra dies and Loas assumes the throne.
- Bisc 2534 -- Kangas' son, Debusis, is born.
- Bisc 2554 -- Kangas dies and Debusis assumes the throne from his father.
- Bisc 2555 -- The twins, Emordra and Ailith, are born.

Acknowledgements

I have always believed in stories, in the role they play in our world and the richness and meaning they bring to our individual lives. On my quest to write and publish this novel, I was fortunate to encounter many angels in the guise of relatives and friends who aided me invariably on this daunting quest. In no special order, my thanks and appreciation goes to the following: Susan Cruise, for believing in me and making me believe that I could become a writer when I was just a mere dreamer; Laura Kopchick, for teaching and equipping me with the necessary elements of craft in your creative writing classes (you're an amazing teacher, attuned to the needs of your students; keep it up); Tram Nguyen, for always being willing to lend an ear to my incessant rants and being the first to sample my ideas; Christina Loteryman, for all your honest criticisms (this book became what it is because of you; I know it still doesn't meet all your standards but at least it's better); Rebekah Mansfield, for your editorial services and acute eye for details (you rock!); Woody Evans, for those memorable evenings we had at the Tarrant County College SE Campus Library (miss you, but I know you are enriching the lives of the students of Zayed University in the UAE some way or the other; keep it up); Jini Sibi, for those wonderful dinners (shhh! don't tell anyone); Mark Bukovich, for those evenings we discussed our writing misadventures and kept hoping; James and Grace Cooper, for every nickel and dime you spent to give me an education (love you!); Christian and Faith NiiAryee, for giving me a new life here in the United States (I couldn't be more grateful); Steven Apell, for being an extraordinary roommate (tu comprende?); Bernice Dahn, for being a wonderful role model in our family (my desire to succeed is built in the fact that I keep looking up to you); My brothers Emmanuel, Godwin, and David, for teaching me that life is not only about pursuing dreams, but also about families; Hercules and Grace Tamakloe, for giving me life (everything I am and would ever be is because of you; rest in peace); Elizabeth, for being a wonderful wife (if I have to choose between you and a billion women in a hundred different lives, I will always choose you!); My cousins, nephews, nieces and uncles, for all those evenings we sat by the fireside dreaming out and telling stories no matter how outrageous they were and losing ourselves in them (it was from those humble beginnings that I learned to become a skillful storyteller; love you all)!

I hope I mentioned everyone. But if I didn't, forgive me and don't take it personal. The most important thing is that you will be in my heart...always!

ABOUT THE AUTHOR

A graduate from the University of Texas, Arlington, Edmund Tamakloe is a freelance writer and blogger. He lives in Arlington, TX with his lovely wife and best friend. Long Live Argalon is his first novel.

23691889R00135

Made in the USA
Charleston, SC
30 October 2013